HARE'S FUR

Trevor Shearston is the author of *Something in the Blood*, *Sticks That Kill*, *White Lies*, *Concertinas*, *A Straight Young Back*, *Tinder*, and *Dead Birds*. His novel *Game*, about the bushranger Ben Hall, was short-listed for the NSW Premier's Literary Awards, Christina Stead Prize for Fiction 2014, long-listed for the Miles Franklin Literary Award 2014, and short-listed for the Colin Roderick Award 2013. He lives in Katoomba, in the Blue Mountains.

Trevor Shearston

HARE'S FUR

SCRIBE

Melbourne • London

Scribe Publications
18–20 Edward St, Brunswick, Victoria 3056, Australia
2 John St, Clerkenwell, London, WC1N 2ES, United Kingdom
3754 Pleasant Ave, Suite 100, Minneapolis, Minnesota 55409, USA

Published by Scribe in Australia and New Zealand 2019
Published by Scribe in North America 2020

Printed and bound in the UK by CPI Group (UK) Ltd, Croydon CR0 4YY

Scribe Publications is committed to the sustainable use of natural resources and the use of paper products made responsibly from those resources.

9781950354122 (US edition)
9781925713473 (Australian edition)
9781925693553 (ebook)

A catalogue record for this book is available from the National Library of Australia

scribepublications.com
scribepublications.com.au

For Bette

The workshop air was clammy with the overnight breath of clay. He walked to the racks and felt the feet of three of the run of bowls he'd thrown a day back. They were close to leather-hard. With the fire, they'd be ready to turn by afternoon. He crouched at the cast-iron stove and laid gumleaves and twigs on the bed of ash and lit a leaf. When the twigs, too, caught, he added pine splits, closed the door, and spun the air vent full open, hearing the sound he'd loved all his life of a fire leaping to obey.

The stove was too slow for coffee, he brewed a pot on the small electric hotplate. The mug was the last he owned of Seth Bligh's high-fired earthenware. It belonged on a safe shelf in the kitchen, but he continued to use it. As Seth would have wanted. *Pots fine enough to keep, cheap enough to drop* had read the sign on his lorry. The man would have been amazed, even horrified, by the price Russell could now ask for a single tea bowl. He drank standing at the window to the right of the wheel and looking out into the bush. Almost everything had finished flowering except for the fringed blue ones that looked like orchids but weren't, and the mountain devils, which put out a few red cups whatever the month. He should have known the name of the blue ones, too, she'd told him more than once. He needed to check the fences around her orchid colonies. And quite suddenly he was in tears, had to stand the mug on the wheel-head and dig in his pocket for a hanky. She would never again paint them, the wallabies could have them. 'No! You damn-well look after them! This afternoon!' He balled the hanky, shoved it back into his pocket.

He went outside to the annexe. Its end wall and half the long side were glass, cobwebbed and spattered, ten glazed doors he'd got cheap at a demolition auction and screwed upright to a timber frame. He walked to the last in the row of bins. He'd checked label and clay yesterday, pinched out a piece and worked it in his fingers. Stored unopened for a year, it was well soured, would hold the big forms he wanted. He pulled out the plastic sheeting he'd tucked loosely back in. The four balls were furred with algae, giant cabbages, their stink rising around him as from a pond stirred with a stick. He clamped a hand each side of the top ball and straightened, spun, and dumped the ball on the wedging table, the pull in his lower back drawing from him a grunt. He dumped the second beside the first, then tucked the plastic tightly around the remaining two balls and lidded the bin.

He had watched Chinese and Japanese potters wedge, and, to satisfy his curiosity, emulated them, but at his own table he wedged as he was taught at sixteen by Seth Bligh, passing on the methods and lore of his native Devon. Five minutes and the clay came alive, had spring under his thumb. He wire-cut and weighed out six three-kilo chunks and kneaded and balled them, rolling each to the back of the table. Then, arms and shoulders needing a rest, he walked to the opening in the side wall and stood breathing white blooms at the bush. He was ageing along with his clays. But he was no longer cold. He returned to the wedging table and made up six more balls, then transferred the balls to boards and began ferrying the loads into the workshop and piling the balls on the benchtop to the right of the wheel. Already he could feel the difference in the air. The pine splits had burned down to ember. He added more, then a chunk of ironbark, and closed the vent to a whisker. He needed the room warm, not hot. He carried the now burbling kettle to the wheel and topped up the slurry bowl into which he'd be dipping his fingers. It was time he settled.

He wanted eight large bottles for the risers directly behind the firebox. He could see the form, the weight towards the foot, yet with shoulders to catch the fly-ash that gusted through the kiln and would melt and run. Thicker walls than he'd usually throw, the heat there massive and prolonged. Half might survive. He'd settle for half.

The wheel stood between the two western windows, in an embayment in the bench. It was his oldest friend. He'd made it himself, at eighteen, its design identical in every respect to Seth

Bligh's, but its timber mountain ash, the staple framing tree at the mill in Blackheath where he'd first encountered the man. He'd replaced the crank and chain, the flywheel bearing twice, and the saddle pad more times than he could remember. But the wheel was the same, his first and only.

He took a dozen plywood batts from the rack where they stood like unsleeved LPs and placed the stack within reach when he sat, then snatched up a handful of clay from the waste bucket on the floor and roughly balled it. He hoisted himself into the saddle and slapped the ball onto the centre of the wheel-head, kicked the bar to set the wheel spinning, and, pushing down and out with his thumbs, worked the clay into a thin pad to take the batts. When it was level he stopped the wheel and picked up a batt and the sponge. He dampened each side and dropped the sponge back in its bucket, then positioned the batt on the pad and hammered around its rim with his fist to seat it.

He swivelled and with both hands lifted the first of his throwing balls and slapped it onto the batt, then set the wheel spinning again and slurried his hands and drew the clay up into a cone, feeling it centre. He pushed down, coned it again, and again pushed down, then opened a well in the clay with his thumbs and formed the floor of the bottle. He inserted the fingers of his left hand into the well and, their pressure opposed by the crook'd index finger of his right on the outside of the ball, pulled the clay up into a thick-walled cylinder, his torso rising in unison on a long slow inbreath, his elbows flaring.

He leaned and reinserted his hand and wrist and repeated the pull, drawing the cylinder higher and thinning the walls, then re-slurried his fingers and on the next pull formed the belly and shoulder and collared the top, leaving enough fatness for the neck. He let the wheel coast and cocked his head and studied belly and shoulder. Satisfied, he drew up the neck and gave it a rolled rim, then reached to the slurry bowl for the strip of soaking chamois to smooth the lip, its touch slicker than any finger.

He slowed the wheel and leaned back and to his right, hands withdrawn, but not yet dismissed. What he'd seen in his mind now existed. He was pleased in particular by the curve of the shoulder, mirrored in reverse where shoulder met neck. 'You'll do,' he said modestly. He brought the wheel to a stop and laid the chamois half-submerged again in the slurry bowl, reached for the wire and made the shrinkage cut between batt and bottle base, then levered the batt from the wheel-head, lifted it in both hands, and, twisting from the waist, slid batt and bottle onto the left-hand wing of the embayment. Twisting right, he plucked the sponge from its bucket and squeezed it out, picked up a fresh batt and dampened its faces, then positioned it on the clay pad and hammered round its rim, so much of his working life this endless unconscious repetition.

He'd been embarrassed the first time a reviewer called his throwing 'masterful'. Adele, though, had protested hotly, 'Of course it is! *And* you know it.' After she retired, she would ask him at breakfast what he was doing that day. If he was going to one of the many jobs she referred to as 'drudge' — blunging clay, mixing and sieving glaze, chipping dags from kiln shelves — he wouldn't see her. But if he was throwing she would get through her watering smartly and arrive at the studio with her knitting and sit in the more comfortable of the two ancient plush armchairs. They would talk companionably between pots, and on into the positioning of the next ball on the wheel-head, but when he began the throw proper, fell into communion with the clay, she would still the needles and her tongue. She was witness to the decades of practice that informed every throw, but had never tired of the magic — the bud-opening of ball into bowl, the shining rise of the cylinder that bellied into a blossom jar. He'd offered once, not long after they were married, to teach her. He still remembered what she'd said in dismissing the offer. *Once I start I might not stop, and we'll have a rivalry on our hands.*

After six bottles his lower back was protesting. He slid backwards from the saddle, put hands on hips and swivelled, feeling the discs crackle. He walked to the stove and floated a hand above the plate, then, keeping his back straight, stooped and spun the vent a turn. It was too soon for another coffee. Instead he filled a mug from the thermos of tank water. He stood sipping while he studied in turn each of the six bottles, looking for the flaw he'd missed when he lifted it from the wheel-head. Only one did his eye return to, the curve of the belly a shade too even. His hands rose towards it, then he lowered them. It wasn't 'bad'. But if when he'd thrown all twelve he had his eight, this would be a cull. The law he lived by was implacable. No glaze, no fire effect, could redeem a dud throw. His gaze went to the two yellowed filing cards pinned on the wall between the windows. He no longer remembered why he'd used a pencil. Probably because in his excitement to get the words down he'd grabbed whatever was to hand.

About form. I am sure that the forms of the most common, everyday utensils can evoke so much that is inexpressible in any other language, about humanness. That with only the very slightest gesture, the merest suggestion of the lip of a jug, or pouring spout, or the lightest softening of a curve, there can be expressed a sort of vulnerability, or a tenderness, or an attentiveness that causes us to pause. That the scale alone of some objects can touch us, and a small jug of open and generous form can somehow seem brave and absurd and a bit like ourselves.

The last words never failed to move him. The second card expressed his own inarticulateness about what he did.

Words get too big. Leave them.

Both quotations were from an essay by Gwyn Hanssen Pigott. He hadn't till then known she could write as well as she threw. He still wondered why, having written the first, she had gone on to write the second. He had also, standing here, wished he'd made the effort to meet her. Too late now. Also dead of a stroke. He closed his eyes, whispered, 'Oh, love.'

He'd been on the wheel, but turning. If throwing, he let the phone ring. He thought it would be Hugh, wanting to pick up the splitter. A woman said, 'Mr Bass?' The reluctance chilled him, made his 'yes' sound cagey even to him.

'Mr Bass, this is Emergency at Katoomba Hospital. We have your wife here and we're —'

'Yes, I'll speak to her please!'

'Your wife's unconscious, Mr Bass. She's had a fall and hit her head.'

'I'll be ten minutes.'

He went as he was, entering the house only to grab his wallet and the ute keys. The receptionist ushered him immediately through triage to a waiting nurse. She conducted him to a cubicle and parted the curtains. Two more nurses and a man in blue surgical gloves glanced round from what they were doing. Breath left him. The nurse cupped his elbow and asked if he needed to sit. He shook his head, but she retained her grip, came with him to the gurney. He didn't recognise the Adele who'd come to the workshop door to say she was going shopping. Her head was encased in bandages, her closed right eyelid and her cheek were black and swollen. A breathing tube was taped into her mouth, thinner tubes ran to and from both forearms. A machine on a stand was emitting a loud beeping. He lifted her limp right hand from the coverlet and enfolded it in both of his. Its coldness terrified him. A chair nudged the backs of his knees. The man came round the foot of the gurney. 'Sit, Mr Bass, please. I'm Dr Dowlan — Edwin.' He had a faint accent Russell did not recognise.

The doctor told him they believed, from what witnesses had told the paramedics, that his wife had suffered a stroke while carrying shopping to her car. Unfortunately, in falling she'd hit her head on a concrete divider. They had not yet done an X-ray, but suspected a skull fracture. He asked what pre-existing medical conditions she had, and Russell told him, Type 2 diabetes. The man frowned. 'Unusual in someone with her light build.'

'Yes.'

'You'd have known, I take it, of the predisposition to stroke?'

'We both did.'

'Of course.'

The X-ray had confirmed the fracture, blood tests the stroke. She'd died that night not knowing he was there.

He could fire the glaze kiln by himself. The tunnel kiln, the anagama, he would never fire again. He couldn't fire it alone, not for seventy hours, and if not with her then not at all. He'd stood at the firemouth a month after she died and spoken the promise aloud.

He threw the rest of the bottles. He squashed three, including the one he'd provisionally sentenced earlier, and dropped their clay in the recycling bin. The remaining nine he transferred to the racks. He checked that the heater had wood, then went outside to the tank and rinsed his hands.

He wasn't especially hungry, but cut bread and cheese and quartered a tomato. He hoped Delys was cooking a roast, not a thing he went to the bother of anymore for just himself. He'd had a second coffee over in the workshop. Another and he'd be flying. He settled for an apple.

He nibbled its last frills of flesh standing on the workshop apron. Once, he'd have then strolled over to the chook run and lobbed the core over the wire to watch the mad scrabble. But only when Adele wasn't home, or he knew he wouldn't be caught. When she still worked it was part of his morning to chuck them a cup of cracked corn and collect the eggs. But they were hers, 'my girls'. Delys had found someone to take them. Partly from guilt he avoided the empty run. A flick of his wrist sent the core bouncing out onto the grass where a currawong would find it.

Keeping an eye on the clock, he turned the feet of the four boards of bowls. After sliding the last board onto its dowels, he ran his eye again along the row of bottles, decided two more might be for the chop.

He took off his clayed trousers on the landing and went inside to the bedroom and pulled on trackpants. The phone rang as he walked back through the kitchen. He let it go to the machine, but stood listening, and whoever it was hung up as soon as his voice started. It used to be hers, and he'd left it for months, the thought of wiping her too painful. In the laundry he took down from the shelf the paintbrush and cloth, then reminded himself aloud that he was going via the orchid colonies and pocketed some twist-ties.

She'd done her doctorate in her early forties, on the biological mechanisms governing fire sensitivity in native terrestrial orchids. They'd travelled together to the south-west of Western Australia, to the Grampians, the Flinders Ranges, Tasmania. They were not places thick with potters, and he let pottery go when they travelled, was content to hunt orchids. But, for him, once to each place was enough. She went alone on the repeat visits timed to the change of seasons and for which she had to apply for study leave, and the adventitious ones following major fires in Gippsland and the Adelaide Hills, which the Gardens were happy to pay for, hoping they would never have to cope with the same catastrophe, but wanting their own expert on hand if ever they did. From plants collected on her trips, and from locally in the Mountains, she had established on their own half-acre colonies of fire-tolerant and fire-loving species to study, photograph, and paint. In the bedroom hung watercolour portraits of spotted doubletails and the large duck orchid, in the kitchen the veined sun orchid, all painted from blooms in the colonies he was walking to. A pad that wound among the trees linked the colonies, starting behind the workshop and merging with the track to what they'd christened, when Michael was a toddler, 'picnic ledge', now anything but that. Most of the species would have died back to their basal leaves, some underground to tubers, but he hadn't inspected the fences since summer and knew himself well enough to know that he might neglect to do so until next summer, when for some it would be too late, their shoots cropped by the resident wallabies.

At the start of the pad, he stopped to pull a cotoneaster and two young holly. Deeper in, the weeds disappeared, shaded out by the thick understorey of tea-tree, acacias, and hakeas, and the even denser ground covers, grevillea laurifolia, dillwynia, hibbertia. The earth was dry and hard, leaves crackling beneath his soles. The first colony was some thirty metres in. Its circular fence of black plastic mesh was intact. It bore no identifying labels — she not needing any — and he no longer remembered what species it enclosed. At the next, a stake had rotted. He found a strong stick and pushed it into the soil and hitched the mesh to it with a twist-tie. The last colony he knew — red beardie — not because it was in flower, but because of its neighbour, a large mountain devil which the wattle birds ransacked in the leaner months, scattering flower debris around its base in a red pool. Nothing of the colony was visible, the plants gone underground. He resisted for once his growing habit of thinking aloud, refusing to be openly maudlin.

He met and turned right onto the track to the ledge, in a couple of minutes crossing the block's invisible boundary and onto National Parks land. As the soil thinned, so did the bush, the blue air over the valley becoming visible between trunks. He walked out onto the ledge, his shadow scattering skinks. The lone leaning banksia that now split the view had been fed on by cockatoos, chewed cones scattered about where the trunk rose so improbably from the crack where once it had been the seedling they'd doubted could survive. Michael had grown faster, but the tree had won.

Watching his feet, not wanting to stumble on a cone, he walked to the edge. The northern skyline was Radiata Plateau, below him the semi-domesticated immensity of the upper Megalong. A column of smoke held his gaze for a moment, then, as they always did, his eyes travelled to the small green square that had been Seth Bligh's home paddock, and the roof set apart from the house that had been his pottery and kiln shed. He had no idea who lived there now. A succession of owners, probably. He'd sometimes had the thought that he should drive down and introduce himself, solve for them the mystery of the shards and wasters that must still litter the place, and the feet-deep midden in the gully behind the shed. Enough, if anyone had the imagination, to pave a sizeable courtyard.

Russell had put that fanciful notion, but not fancifully, to Adele when a Cultural Centre and Gallery was announced for the old TAFE site. It was a lovely and loyal idea, she'd told him, but would he please, for both their sakes, not take it any further. He hadn't. But he'd stood on the lake of grey concrete the Centre's architects called a courtyard.

The ledge was accessible only through his land. At the split in its southern end he halted and looked about him, without reason, but here the instinct for privacy was strong. He gripped the knob of rock on which years of her hand and his had left a low polish, dropped onto the first of the four boulders he'd placed himself as steps, and descended to the second ledge, roofed by the one he'd just walked over.

The two urns stood half a metre apart on a low table of ferric-red flowstone. Michael they had placed at the far end, leaving room for two more. Adele was at the centre, her rightful place. Where he would stand was marked, for Hugh's benefit, with a quartz pebble. They were his joint executors, Hugh and Delys, but Delys had told him bluntly she wouldn't ever be setting foot here. The lid and shoulders of each pot were white with the stone powder that fell as a constant drizzle from the overhang roof. Michael's was a high-shouldered blossom jar in the temmoku he was using back then. It was made lidless, but when he and Adele had walked into the workshop the morning after the funeral to choose a vessel into which to pour their son, their eyes had gone to the same pot. He had, defying his dislike of them, given it lugs. He wondered still if he'd attached the lugs knowing they'd be needed. Three cords of plaited copper wire, whipped at the lugs and where they met, held down the brass lid.

Adele's urn was the guan jar that had stood for years in the bedroom, its form not exceptional, but the subtleties of grey in the glaze, and its pearl opacity, making it one of the finest guans ever to have come from the kiln. That, too, had been a surreal morning, sitting at the kitchen table and spooning her into the jar from the plastic box in which she'd come from the undertakers', then squeezing a worm of silicon around the rim and pressing the lid into place. He had, of course, thought about what glaze human ash might give. It had none of the fluffiness of wood ash. This was coarse and heavy, rattled against the jar's sides. The word that had entered his mind was 'slag', quickly pushed away.

His own urn he had not yet lifted from the kiln. The day of their joining he *had* seen, though. An autumn morning a thousand, two thousand years from now — and early, first light. The brief tinkle of shattering ceramic lost in the roar of collapsing stone, the three of them drifting down to be earth together. He didn't believe — as Delys did — that the vision was morbid. If anything, the opposite.

He cleaned Michael first, pressing with the point of his index finger on the lid to keep the jar steady while he brushed. The brass had grown a green patina as beautiful as any glaze.

When Adele, too, was clean, her glaze lustrous, he stepped to the edge and held the cloth out into the stream of cold air rising from the valley and beat it free of powder with the flat of the brush, then folded the cloth and pushed it and the brush into his pocket. He turned again to the jars, and his eyes filled. He closed them, ashamed to look at her.

'I know, the worst addiction, self-pity.'

The walk to Hugh and Delys's was thirty minutes using his short cut. He drove only when it was raining. He pulled the front door closed, glanced at his watch — ten to six — at the sky smeared with high pink cloud, then set off across the grass towards the gap in the belt of natives that was the front fence she'd planted, the bottle of merlot in his daypack bumping pleasantly on his spine. When they'd first seen this house it was alone, the road dirt, more a track, running to a lookout not maintained since the thirties. Trees now hid the view from its platform, roots had cracked and tilted the concrete. Once or twice a month a car would arrive, lured by the map, but those who got out didn't stay long. Photographs of the lookout in its prime, however, before the first war, showed women in long dresses and wide plumed hats posed with men in tight pinstriped suits and bowlers, every man wearing a handlebar moustache. The road was now coarse bitumen, and the house was no longer alone.

As he came abreast of the nearest of his neighbours, Helen Kent and her kids, he heard a rhythmic thudding. The son, Jerome, on his drum kit. It was the same 4/4 beat he'd heard before, seemingly all the boy knew, but he appeared to be improving, the strokes more confident. Helen had asked once if 'the noise', as she'd put it, bothered him. Quite the opposite, he'd answered truthfully. Adele had started Michael on the violin. He'd progressed to simple pieces before the chemo made him too weak to hold the instrument. Violin had been the obvious choice because she could teach him. But with a greater say — or any — might he too have chosen drums? There had been few rock records in the house, a couple of Bob Dylans, some early Rolling Stones and Beatles, his, not Adele's. The collection she'd brought to the marriage was entirely classical. Oistrakh and Menuhin were the masters Michael had imbibed with his mother's milk. He consciously listened again as he left the drumming behind. Still the relentless 4/4, using bass drum and the hard rattly one. Snare! Of course, fife and snare. The instruments of Waterloo. And New Orleans. He wondered if the boy would ever hear any swing.

On Narrow Neck Road he walked into a light mist. He would need his ears tuned when he reached the tracks. He crossed the highway on the overpass — cars hissing below, their lights on — and descended the cutting on the concrete strip that sealed its rim. Pines made it almost gloomy enough for his torch. He found the break in the railway's fence and ducked through and was now officially trespassing. He pushed through waist-high coral fern down to the tracks and walked out onto the ballast. The cutting amplified any train approaching from the west. To the east, even with the mist, he could see. He committed, did a fast skip across both pairs of rails. A dirt track followed the fence down to West Street, then up the lane to Mort and on past the deserted oval. The front of the house was in darkness, he was expected at the back. In the side passage he walked into the glorious smell of roasting lamb!

The door was the original laundry's, opening directly into the long narrow kitchen. He didn't knock. Tom, their Maltese terrier, had heard him, though, and was waiting. He gave a single woof of welcome and danced about Russell's feet. The air was hazed with lamb fat and, after the air outside, almost stifling. Delys turned from the sink with tomatoes in her hand. 'Good evening.'

'And very good to be spending it here.'

He stood at the end of the island bench and thumbed off the straps of the daypack. Neither was a person who felt the need to rush to the other for the customary kiss. He extracted the bottle and placed it without fanfare on the benchtop. Only then did he walk to her. She was slicing. She offered her cheek, and he planted a kiss. Her skin and hair, too, were lamb-scented. She pointed past him with the ancient non-stainless but razor-edged knife she used for everything. 'Pop those in now, so you don't forget.' An egg carton with the added precaution of a rubber band sat on the counter beside the fridge.

'Forget? When I know how badly you need the money!'

She laughed. 'Just do it, you nong.'

'Hey!' But he dug in his pocket and lifted the carton and left in its place a small pyramid of coins. From the pack he took an empty carton, slid the full one in, placed the empty beside the coins.

'I trust, carrying those, you're taking the *sensible* way home?'

'I *am.*'

'But you came over the line.'

'Del, as I'm at pains to point out every time we have this argument, you can hear, and you can see. You simply walk across.'

'I'll quote that at your funeral, shall I?'

They were old sparring partners. On this subject he'd invariably faced two, her and Adele. It had been weirdly like arguing with twins — Delys, Adele — but for the fact that they looked so different, Adele small and neatly made, Delys big, with carroty curls only now beginning to grey and lose their spring.

Hugh bustled through the door from the lounge room. 'Break it up, you two.' He slid conciliatory fingers along her cheek as he passed. The two men embraced, Hugh keeping his face a careful distance from Russell's. His beard smelled of the gumleaves he'd used to start the fire. 'It's cool out there, old son.

Soon be able to light up a kiln with impunity.' He lifted the bottle and looked at the label. 'We had this before?'

'Not from me. The bloke in the Cellars assured me it's good.'

'Only one way to find out.' He halted on his way to the dresser. 'Or would you prefer to start with a beer?'

'No, that.'

'My sweet?' Hugh said, displaying the bottle. 'Or you want to stick with the white?'

She'd finished the tomatoes and started on a cucumber. 'The white,' she said, not looking up.

'Do I have time to show the man something?'

'If you had any sense of time. Set the table, both of you, please.'

Russell carried cork mats and placemats, Hugh the cutlery. The dining table shared the big living room. Pots — some Russell's — sat on every shelf, filled the mantelpiece, squatted in corners. A backlog from the borer-riddled wattle Hugh had dropped in their yard was well ablaze, propped on two molten chunks of ironbark. Even from over at the table Russell felt the heat. The gooseneck lamp in the corner was off, but the board and pieces were set up on the low blackwood table, their two chairs drawn up ready. Both returned to the kitchen for further orders.

They were family, there was no palaver of pre-dinner snacks. Hugh bore in the roast, Russell the cast-iron baking dish of spuds and pumpkin, Delys the salad and gravy. The salad bowl, gravy boat, and plates were a Gulgong proto-porcelain called Ming 60, long ago mined out. Russell had never liked or worked in porcelains, found them cold, but this set broke his rule. The salted surfaces had a glow, flame-paths were flashed a subtle pink. He had been coming here long enough to have 'his' plate. He ran a finger lightly round its rim to feel the fineness of the salting, before lifting the plate for Hugh to lay on it the slices speared on the carving fork.

He ate two mouthfuls of meat before touching anything else, then, knife and fork raised in exclamation, said, 'Del — this lamb's superb.'

'And so is your wine.'

They exchanged nods, and the light rift was healed.

Hugh reached to the salad bowl and pinged the rim with a fingernail. 'This's long gone, as you know. But what I wanted to show you, Home Rule's sent me a sample bag of a body they reckon flashes. It's as fine as this, throws a bit like it. I can hope.'

'What are they calling it?' Russell asked, unable to disguise the prickliness that entered his tone. *Heal one rift*, he thought, *open another.*

'Yes, they're being a bit naughty. Hmong.'

'That doesn't even make sense. It sounds Burmese.'

Hugh laughed uneasily. 'If it salts and it flashes they can call it "billygoat" for all I care!'

Hugh had never dug and processed his own clays. His reason, expressed early in their friendship, was the unlikelihood of finding a good salting body by chance, and locally. Russell had soon learned the true reason, that Hugh, though a lovely thrower, was not an experimenter, hadn't the patience. Russell stopped inviting him on forays to creeks and road cuttings. Hugh had his clays delivered, ready to throw, to the studio door. Yet — a seeming paradox — he had always shared, even surpassed, Russell's fascination with firewoods, the different ash colours and effects produced by different timbers. The same tree lopper supplied them both. The upper Mountains were full of pines past their prime and threatening houses or falling across roads. They jointly owned the pneumatic splitter mounted on a trailer body and towed to one or the other yard when needed. The time Hugh tripped over the dog and broke his wrist halfway through a restaurant order, Russell had completed the throwing and glazing, and they'd fired the salt kiln together. Without Hugh and Delys, Russell would have, in the first months after her death, gone mad with grief. It was Delys who quietly removed from the fridge Adele's insulin, knowing the use it could be put to. Now she lifted the tongs and pincered a pair of potato halves and deposited them on his plate. 'Before Hugh scoffs them all.'

'I beg your pardon!'

For answer she plucked up a half and dropped it on her husband's plate.

'They're good spuds,' Russell said. 'What sort are they?'

'"Scoffs"!' Hugh snorted.

She ignored him. 'Dutch Creams. You can get them at the co-op. Nicer than Pontiacs. I think, anyway.'

When they were eating again Russell asked, not out of politeness but genuine interest, what she was working on. She was, or had been — would fully retire if she could finally get publishers to believe her — a freelance editor, exclusively of non-fiction, for preference history and biography. He too read no fiction, having decided early in life that real people and events were far too interesting to bother with the invented.

'A biog of Ho Chi Minh. A translation from French.'

Russell smiled. 'Is there anything in it you didn't already know?'

'Quite a bit, actually. The writer's Vietnamese.'

'Did you know he was a potter?' Hugh said.

'What?' Russell flicked his gaze from one to the other. There was no telltale smirk. 'Really?'

'No,' Delys said. 'But he kept a lot of potters in work making and firing those giant urns they buried rice in to hide it.' She opened her mouth to add something, then clapped it shut and stood and grabbed up the empty salad bowl. 'You two start, I'll bring dessert.'

She was at the doorway to the kitchen when Russell realised what her awkwardness had been. *Urns.*

Hugh switched on the lamp and bent the neck to shrink the pool of light to the perimeter of the board. They didn't use a timer. The game fell into its usual pattern of rapid, almost automatic, opening gambits followed by a slowing as their styles and strategies diverged. Delys brought them stewed plums and cream. Each man received his bowl distractedly, one eye still on the board. But they were not so distracted, or unwise, as to forget to murmur thanks. She stood a moment and studied the position of the pieces but offered no comment. In all the years he'd known her, Russell had never seen her play. It frustrated Hugh that she preferred to read. When the two of them travelled, she played to stop his badgering. Russell had learned not to ask after their return from a trip how many times she'd beaten him. She laid an affectionate hand — or was it 'good luck, my sweet, you're already in trouble' — on her husband's nape, then went to the fire and took up the poker and hooked the backlog forward into the ember, hunted the dog from her chair.

Hugh's playing was learned, Russell's intuitive. Neither commanded a habitual superiority. And one of them usually prevailed. But after two hours the game was a futile pursuit, the black king defended by a rook and a few hapless pawns, the white by the same number of pawns and a knight. 'Quits?' Hugh said. Russell nodded. Hugh reached to the baize-lined box sitting on the sill and set it on the table.

Delys marked her place, and all three adjourned to the kitchen. Hugh went to the machine, she filled the jug. Russell perched on a stool. Hugh made two strong flat whites while Delys brewed Hugh a camomile. Not sleeplessness but his bladder wouldn't permit him coffee at night. Seeming not to remember that he always said the same thing, he said, 'I don't know how you two can do it.'

Delys slipped Russell a wink. 'A solid early addiction, my darling.' Russell laughed. But for him it was close to the truth. Seth Bligh had despised tea, kept a once-blue but thoroughly blackened enamel coffee pot permanently on the stove in his workshop.

Hugh was yawning behind his fist. Russell drained his cup. 'I'll head off.'

'I don't suppose there's any point offering a lift?'

Russell shaded his eyes to look through the room's reflection into the yard. There was moonlight on the leaves of the black bamboo beside the workshop.

'Your brew'll power me home.'

He embraced each. Delys said, looking into his eyes, 'She's still very much in our thoughts.'

'I know.'

Hugh lifted the daypack from the floor and held the straps for him to insert his arms.

'When do you need the splitter?' Russell said. 'I'm still a month or more away.'

'I mightn't. Got a good bit stacked. Not in your road, is it?'

'No. And I'm thinking I'll go down the valley tomorrow. The usual, I'll ring that I'm back. So, next week. Or sooner if you want the splitter.' He wouldn't see Delys, she stayed home and read. He reached for and squeezed her hand, the words she'd spoken still between them. The dog, too, was waiting to say goodbye. Russell ruffled the thinning hair on the scalp, drew his fingers up one velvet ear.

He had returned to his young man's habit of sleeping with the curtains open, was up before the sun. He filled a glass at the sink and stood as he did every morning, absently drinking while looking out to judge how cold it had got, what the sky promised. Rags of mist hung in the gums behind the workshop. The grass sparkled, again only with dew. But his breath was visible, made a circle on the pane. The small blow heater she'd insisted on buying for the kitchen was still where it lived, behind the pantry door. He hated the noise of the thing. A month or so, though, and he'd be forced to bring it out in the mornings. He turned mechanically to the row of saucepans hung from hooks before his mind's voice cut in, said not to waste time on porridge. Throw the teapots he'd agreed to, then get down to the creek. He fried two of Delys's eggs.

The air in the workshop was cold, his breath pluming, but he didn't go immediately to the stove, he went instead to the racks and felt the feet of two of the bottles. Not ready — he could do just the teapots and leave. He couldn't do anything, though, until he'd lit a fire, and had a coffee. He used bark and twigs, added pine splits and, when they were ablaze, a light chunk of yellow box. Starved of air, a small fire would be safe to leave.

He brewed the pot on the electric hotplate, drank it from Seth's mug. Then he went out to the annexe. He'd promised four, would throw eight. He wedged and balled the clay and carried the balls, and a larger ball for the spouts and lids, piled on one board, back to the workshop. He'd stopped making teapots — too fiddly and time-consuming, and the form itself had lost its interest — but the unspoken bargain with Geoffrey at Clay was that he agreed to the occasional group show in return for his solo ones. Not that he any longer needed the money from either. The house was years ago paid off, he qualified for a part-pension, and her superannuation resided now in his account, far more than he could envisage ever spending. He'd had the same conversation with Hugh, that when they were younger and really needed to sell what they produced, they couldn't get prices that gave them a living. Both were forced to teach. Now, their reputations made, they could command the prices but no longer needed the money. He remembered the curl of Hugh's lip. 'Tell them all to get fucked, shall we, and retire!'

He threw a full-bellied teapot, then measured and threw its lid, set each on a batt and pulled from the larger ball a chunk and balled it in his hands, and threw a spout. He cut the spout from the wheel and stood it upright beside the pot, to attach tomorrow. He was aware as he threw that he wasn't totally engaged, in a part of his mind already down in the valley. Even so he made no mistakes, at the end of two hours had eight he could live with.

His old canvas A-frame hung with the hats on the row of hooks on the landing wall. He carried it into the kitchen and sat it on a chair and went to the bedroom, returned wearing his down jacket. He made a plunger and filled the slim hiking thermos and stood it in the pack. He washed an apple and a pear, wrapped them in a tea towel and pushed the bundle into the pack to jam the thermos upright. A handful of dates, another of almonds he dropped into a clickseal pouch, which he pushed into the side pocket of his jacket. He drew the pack's drawstrings, but didn't tie them. He hoisted the pack by its straps and walked out to the landing and sat on the woodbox and put on his boots. The cherrywood staff she'd bought him for his seventieth beckoned from the corner of the landing. He turned and went down the steps and walked across the grass to the annexe. The folded leather ore bags were on the bench beside the ball mill, the geologists' pick on top. He worked the bags through the mouth of the pack, then pushed the pick handle down beside the thermos till the head nestled on the bags. He tied the drawstrings and buckled the flap, then shouldered the straps and walked along the corridor between the kilns, the most direct route to the road.

He was going into the valley to the head of a nameless creek where, at a dyke, he filled one of the leather ore bags with decomposing basalt. Crushed and ball-milled and fluxed with ash from the workshop stove, the stone gave him a fat and very black temmoku breaking to rust or sometimes to a piercing blue, or, when saggared for heavier reduction, the streaks of brown called hare's fur. The second ore bag he filled with splinters he broke with the pick from a seam of milky-green rock which, fluxed with the same ash, gave him the unctuous grey-white called guan that somewhere in every firing blushed a delicate pink he'd never sought to analyse, but simply accepted as a gift.

The walk was work, but it was also a meditation. After she retired Adele had occasionally come with him. Then it was not a meditation but a continuation of the long conversation that was their marriage. And it was slower going, especially in spring, for she was constantly darting off into the bush to photograph a possumwood in flower, or an orchid she'd spotted. He was generous with what he'd learned in the fifty-six years since he'd thrown his first pot. To a fault, as she'd many times told him. But he had never publicly disclosed the source of his two signature glazes. Nor had he ever invited Hugh to come with him, and Hugh, knowing why, had never invited himself. For he had found the dyke and the seam on one of the solitary grieving walks he'd done, incapable of work, after Michael's death. The creek was a place he could share only with Adele. Now, no one.

Tea-tree and lomandra had grown across the opening of the abandoned lookout. He pushed through the clumps of blades to the apron of lichened concrete and found the faint pad that only his feet maintained, skirting to the right of the platform through wind-sculpted casuarinas and hakea and more tea-tree to the cliff edge. There he stopped and removed his beanie and took the sun on his face and scalp. It was the last direct sunlight he would know until he stood again on this spot. He put his beanie back on, then, parting the shrubs like a swimmer, advanced till he was at the top of the near-vertical cleft that some fool many years ago had christened, in lead undercoat, Devil's Well.

After thirty or so of the deep stone steps his knees began to jelly, but he resisted reaching to the rusted chain laced to the cliff face, not trusting the ancient concrete that plugged the piton holes. A trickle of water entered invisibly on his left, its tinkle the only sound but for that of his boots and his breathing. Cold air rose up the cleft as if up a ventilator shaft, carrying the paradoxical odours of mossed stone and dust. A yellow-breasted robin joined him, flittering above the rasp ferns. The bird stayed close, hunting for moths or flies disturbed by his passage. Russell didn't see it take one, and near the bottom of the cleft, where the glen widened, it gave up and disappeared, the air too cold yet for insect wings. The widening was a stone patio that looked down into the continuation of the glen. The slab had once slid from the rock face, but would slide no further, staked in place by three massive coachwoods, their bark grown onto the stone. The trickle was louder, further down becoming a creek, which was joined by another running from the falls below his house and on down to the valley floor to be met by 'his' creek.

He halted and dug the fingertips of both hands hard into the hollows of his right knee. From somewhere below, sounding closer in the cold air than they probably were, a male and female whipbird were doing their antiphonal trick, the call and response like a single bird. He could mimic the whistles of rosellas, bring them to the wattle behind the kilns peering down at him in bewilderment. But this call was impossible. He bent and straightened his knee, then started down the scree.

He followed the creek now, the light a deep green, the track almost obliterated by the ploughing of lyrebirds. He'd been here so many times he recognised individual trees. When he reached the junction he stood looking up into the jumble of car-sized boulders from beneath which 'his' creek emerged. The ford was a line of mossed stones where the creeks joined. Two-thirds across he crouched to drink, the water tasting like licked steel. Still crouched, he reached into the flow and picked up one of the black pebbles that so long ago had told him that a strongly iron-bearing rock was shedding into the creek. He could have made a load from the pebbles scattered in the shallows, but that would have meant a wet ore bag. Anyway, he had to walk in to the seam that gave him his guan. He rose and stepped the last three stones to the tiny beach. Against the bank was a black log once adzed flat for a seat. Terraces of orange fungi climbed its sides, rotted wood spilled from its heart. He propped on his buttocks and pulled from his pocket the pouch and ate two dates and some almonds. A sign once nailed to a coachwood now leaned against its base, the words illegible but the arrow chiselled in the timber still visible. One day to satisfy his curiosity he'd obeyed the arrow and found that a junction with the well-used and maintained National Parks track to Helga Falls was only ten minutes away. He stepped round to the back of the log and parted the callicoma growing in a curtain. Here started the pad that ran up the left-hand side of the creek and on which he'd never seen a boot print other than Adele's or his own.

The pad climbed on tree roots to a low ridge, dropped to the creek, then climbed again steadily into the boxed canyon until he came in sight of what he called the 'cape', a bluff of raw sandstone, with caves and overhangs visible around its base. He'd never had the inclination to explore them. If Michael had lived they might have done it together. Rocks from its face had tumbled as far as the creek bed and in places offered the only, but unstable, footing — why he was watching where he placed his feet.

And so saw it, lying between two rocks, a wrapper. A lolly wrapper.

He halted and stared, not quite believing his eyes, then bent awkwardly in the pack and plucked it up. It was so new it crackled. Mars bar. The crimped seal was intact, the cellophane ripped open in a ragged spiral. He raised it to his nose. The smell of chocolate was fresh. But the white inner skin, he saw, had a sheen of moisture. The wrapper had lain overnight. Currawongs picked up shiny things, but would have discarded this as useless long before flying over here. From a light plane, then? Or a chopper? Both crisscrossed the valleys. He knew he was clutching at straws. The wrapper had been dropped from a hand. But going where? There was nowhere. To the head of a nameless creek at the end of a blind canyon. Without a reason like his who would bother?

He crumpled the wrapper, but it refused to ball. He stuffed the springy thing into his jacket pocket — and froze when there came the ring of something hollow and metal against stone, followed by a shrill giggle, a child's.

He held his breath but the giggling didn't come again. He breathed into his palm while he slowly swivelled his head. But both sounds, he was sure, had come from just upstream. There was a small pool on the other side of a fall of boulders that had, eons ago, partly dammed the creek. On days in December and January he'd sat on its gravel beach and paddled his feet. Even in midsummer the water numbed them in seconds, his boots feeling weirdly too big when put back on. No one could be paddling at this time of year.

He pulled off his beanie and stuffed it in his pocket, the grey of his hair less conspicuous. Then he chose a route, marking to himself rocks that looked wedged. Using fingertips as feelers he crept up the dam wall, every few steps cautiously straightening to determine whether he could see the pool.

The giggle came again, more subdued, and again he froze. It was followed by a voice, answered by another. Both voices were young, but the second older than the first. He couldn't make out words, but they carried the earnest tone of children deciding rules. There came the hollow clunk of a stone dropped into what might have been a kettle. He heard the metal thing scrape, then a light splash. He couldn't just stand guessing. He hunched and in five careful steps reached the spillway down which the water from the pool fell. He slowly raised his head and through the leaves of a shrub got a glimpse of a yellow shirt or jacket, and above it something red, a cap or beanie. If he climbed a further step, keeping the same shrub between him and the pool, a rock bare of moss would give him a clearer view. The pack was unbalancing him. He carefully shrugged the straps from his shoulders and lowered the pack into a cleft between his feet, testing that it was jammed before lifting his hand. He ducked his head and placed his foot and brought the other to meet it, then laid both hands flat on the boulder from which the shrub appeared to grow, and levered himself up, not sure how close he would find himself to the speakers.

They were on their haunches on the hump of rock which divided the beach, the width of the pool between them and him. The shrub's foliage was sufficiently dense that he had to sway his head to see. The owner of the shriller voice was a boy about five. The other was a girl he guessed to be eight or nine. Both wore trackpants and cheap unpadded windcheaters, the boy's yellow, the girl's blue. The windcheaters were filthy. He was reminded of the engrained filth in the windcheaters of the men and women who rummaged through bins in Katoomba Street. A small aluminium saucepan with string tied to the hole in its handle floated at a listing angle on the pool. The other end of the string was in the boy's hand. The stone he'd heard dropped into metal had been, he guessed, to correct a worse list. The gazes of both were locked on the saucepan. It drifted for a moment before the current caught it, carrying it towards a log around which the water purled.

'Pull it, you little shit!' the girl ordered.

The boy instead paid out slack, allowing the saucepan to sail further into danger. But when she half-rose he gave the string a delicate, practised jerk, and the saucepan spun out of the current and back towards the beach. She thrust out her hand for the string.

'Give it.'

He'd been intrigued by the game, but now he studied the faces. They lacked the roundness of children's faces, looked bony, underfed. The boy was olive-skinned, his cheeks burnished like — again — those of the bin-rummagers in town, and probably from the same cause, sun and wind. Enough of his hair showed from under the beanie to reveal that it was dark brown. The girl's face, by contrast, was pale, almost drawn. She was bareheaded and blonde. He had assumed from her coarse familiarity that they were brother and sister, but now was less sure.

She leaned and snatched the string and he saw that behind her, lying on its side, was a blue plastic nine-litre bucket, its handle lashed to a thick stick snapped at both ends. They weren't on a picnic. He looked beyond them, searching for a shape or colour that might be a tent. There wasn't one, or it was out of sight. His gaze returned to the puzzle of the bucket. You didn't carry a bucket to camp overnight. On foot, you didn't carry one at all, or if you did, a canvas one, not rigid plastic. Both of them looked to be school-age, but the girl certainly. As far as he knew it wasn't holidays. Not for the Kent kids anyway. The day before yesterday he'd passed them coming home on their bikes, both in uniform.

The girl was bringing the saucepan in hand over hand, like landing a fish. The game was over, he hoped — they'd fill the bucket and go. He could watch where they went. The parent was a fool, sending a boy this size to be on the other end of nine litres of water. And for walking past the creek junction, water at your door, to pitch camp somewhere in a jumble of boulders and forest. The girl was lifting the saucepan from the water. He waited for her to tip out the stones. Instead she held the saucepan level and reached in. She was adjusting the ballast. She bent again to the surface of the pool and relaunched the saucepan, a controlled flick sending it out towards the current while she paid out string. He lowered his head, said into his chest, 'Shit!' A splash made him look up. The boy had fired a pebble whose ripples were rocking the saucepan, and would have fired another except that the girl slapped it from his fingers.

'Don't. I didn't spoil yours.'

'But you're havin two!' the boy whined.

She ignored him and whipped the wet string to turn the handle to face upstream. Would the game go on until whoever needed the water came looking for them? The only way of getting upstream was past the pool. Not that he'd explored alternative routes, never having had to. But the canyon was too narrow for there to be any — none, certainly, where he'd be both unseen and unheard. He could crab to his left, then stand. But they would bolt, he was sure, the second he showed himself. It was the feral in their appearance, the filthy windcheaters, the slightly starved faces. And they were too at ease, like kids playing in their own backyard. They would react as if to an intruder. Which he was. If they were actually living close by.

He glanced up towards the cape, but most of it was hidden by the upper branches of the shrub he was using as a screen. The logical place was one of the caves. But who would bring children to live in a cave? And why! Clearly they didn't want to be discovered, whoever they were. Perhaps desperately didn't want to be. Even if he waited for the children to tire of their game and fill the bucket and leave, he couldn't continue on to the head of the creek and blithely start chopping stone. The ring of hardened steel would bring him company in no time. His obvious age, and the innocence of his reason for being there, might not be adequate against someone too crazy or too frightened to believe him. And a geologist's pick, although a perfectly good tool, would make a clumsy weapon.

The boy was whining again to be given a turn. If he waited, maybe whoever was on top might come looking, or at least yell.

He'd know, then, who he faced. But that still didn't mean he'd be able to fill his bags.

'You can't,' he whispered. 'Not today, anyhow.'

Frustrating, though, to have to repeat the walk. And how many days should he wait before trying again? They might still be here. He levered himself up and studied the intent faces with a matching intensity, not sure why, but wanting them imprinted on his memory. He closed his eyes, checked that he had them, looked at them again, it only now occurring to him that they were not so feral that they sensed being watched.

The girl paused in drawing on the string to blow a strand of hair from her left eye rather than brush it with wet fingers. Despite the game she was engaged in, her air of calmness was adult. In the second half of his life he'd had little to do with children. Had they perhaps all grown more self-assured? Well, Helen's two hadn't. The boy — Jerome — was older than this girl, but wouldn't meet his eye when he spoke to him and, according to his mother, was terrified of the dark. He'd perhaps misjudged the parent here. These two seemed not at all fearful — of being out in the bush, or of what, down here, would be pitch-dark nights, just a slit of sky. They obviously felt themselves safe, whatever the reason for being here. He shouldn't destroy that feeling.

He took a last look. The girl had pulled the saucepan boat to the beach. She unlooped the string from her fingers and passed

the coil to the boy. Russell looked behind his feet for the rock
he'd stepped up from.

He came round the side of the house and the forty metres
further to the annexe looked a long way. The ore bags could stay
in the pack until morning. He took off his boots and knocked
them together above the herb bed, then, carrying them,
climbed the steps in his socks. A small but perfect butternut
pumpkin sat on the bamboo stool, holding down a note. He
knew who they were from, and what the note would say.

The invitation was to dinner. *If he was free.* He was always
both touched and irritated by the phrase. She'd have warned
whichever of the kids was her messenger not to disturb him at
the workshop. He walked to the phone and looked at the list
taped to the wall and dialled. The girl answered.

'Hello Lucy, it's Russell.'

'I'll get her.'

When Helen came on he thanked her for the pumpkin and
the invite. Unfortunately, though, he'd just got back from one
of his trips down into the valley, why she'd not heard from him
earlier. He hoped she hadn't started cooking, he'd been planning
just to have a bath and a boiled egg and fall into bed. No, she
said. She'd just thought, being the end of the week, he might
like to share 'a relaxing glass'. He'd told her before that he didn't
have a working week, his cycles were firings. Not strictly the

truth, he reminded himself — when Adele still worked they'd taken some note of Fridays — but the truth now.

'How about tomorrow or Sunday? It's just we haven't seen you in a bit.'

He knew what she was doing, repaying her debt to Adele by keeping an eye on him, and he allowed it — as much as he could stand anyway before forbearance crossed over into annoyance. Adele had introduced her to painting, and changed, even perhaps saved, her life. The reason for her persistence now, though, he knew, wasn't just gratitude. She'd finished a new painting. When Adele was alive, she'd been her sounding board. But Helen knew he'd performed the same role for Adele, as she had for him. *That*, he missed exquisitely, unpacking the kiln together, discussing the merits or faults of a pot held in gloved hands, the glaze still softly pinging as it cooled and crackled. Adele had started Helen in her own field, still lifes, but the woman had quickly outgrown watercolour and started in oils. Her confidence soon matched her growing skills. She began painting what she called 'psychological landscapes'. The few he saw he'd found technically accomplished but turgid. Adele, though, had more sympathy for what the woman was trying to do. 'She's painting what she's feeling, Russell. And if she persists she'll paint herself *out* of what she's feeling.'

The Kents had arrived in the house across the road six years ago, with two then small children. He was a civil engineer with the biblical name Gideon. Russell and Adele saw little of him, work took him away for weeks at a time. But when home he was friendly enough, asking Adele's advice on what natives to plant and taking an engineer's interest in the kilns. A year after their arrival a bridge had taken him to Thailand, and he hadn't come back.

'Um — can we say Sunday? And what time would you like me?'

'Early's fine. Six? Don't bring anything, just yourself.'

'You sure?'

'Absolutely! Please.'

He hung up, then stood, seeing in his mind the seconds shelf in the workshop. He had five teacups he'd saved to refire. He'd give them a wash, choose one. He picked up the phone again, dialled from memory. Hugh answered.

'You're back. How are the knees?'

'A bit crunchy. I'm going to give them a soak.'

If he said he had to go down again, he'd have to explain. Leave it a fortnight and he wouldn't.

'You got Tiger?'

'I can't use it! I've told you. The damn stuff burns.'

'It's *supposed* to! How it works.'

'Well, I'm not giving it the chance.'

'Suffer, then.'

'Thank you.'

He put on Arvo Pärt's *Alina* and lit the heater, ran a bath. He left the bathroom door open. He wet a flannel under the cold tap and enfolded his balls and cock, then slowly lowered himself into the steaming water and sat with his legs straight. The water was too hot, but he made himself be still, his mind on the music, and after a couple of minutes his legs could bear it. With his fingertips he began to massage the sides of each knee in turn. And as he'd known they would, the children came.

Where would they be right now? 'Not in a hot bath, that's certain.' If they were washing at all it would be in the pool. They wouldn't be washing, it was getting dark. Hopefully they'd be sitting round a fire. Eating what, though? Chocolate bars? He closed his eyes and looked at their pinched faces. They couldn't have been living down there long enough, they must already have looked like that, or half like that. He'd been to garage sales on the town's northern side, dead fridges and washing machines in the front yards, cars on bricks in driveways. The cops would probably know who they were, might even be looking for them. The last people he'd tell. If it was a woman escaping some bastard bashing her, why hadn't she gone to the Women's Centre? No matter how terrified you were, it wasn't fair to young kids to drag them down to a place like that. Just the walk was enough without making them lug things like saucepans and buckets. And where were they getting food? Or was Mars bars all they'd taken?

He opened his eyes. 'They're not your worry. And she won't welcome knowing they've been spotted.'

He made himself listen to the piano trickling through the doorway, the clarity of each note in the tiled room. But his mind refused to stop. When he got out he'd be putting on his heavy jumper and heating up soup to have in front of the news, then into bed under a doona. They'd be sleeping in their clothes. In bags if they were lucky, but more likely blankets, and thin ones.

'Listen, they were playing boats. That's hardly a sign of desperation.'

He cupped water and sluiced the sweat from his face, then stood and stepped out onto the mat, not reaching immediately for the towel, letting his skin cool. The mirror was too steamed to see himself, but he addressed the shape there.

'They're skinny, yes, but they didn't look sick, or like they've been knocked around. Go down in a week and they'll be gone. It's not your mystery to solve.'

The heater had taken the chill off the living room. He stoked it, then went to the kitchen and took the pot of soup from the fridge, set it on the front burner, and cut two slices of bread and stood them in the toaster. The words rose up from his childhood, *give us this day our daily bread.* He laid the bowl in his hand back down and went to the drawer below the phone and brought out the book, carried it to the table.

He knew the acronym, a very public history of stuff-ups and heavy-handedness had made it notorious. So much so, he discovered, that the body had been relabelled. *Formerly Department of Community Services. See Family and Community Services.* He turned to the new listing. There was a helpline.

43

To report child abuse and neglect. 24 hours. He stared at the words. Did they describe what he had witnessed? Two children playing in a creek with a saucepan? Whoever came wouldn't settle for having the creek pointed out on a map. He'd have to be prepared to lead welfare officers, or even police, down to the pool. It wasn't certain that the person with them was a woman. Too many disturbed men waving a knife or a lump of wood had been shot dead. He closed the book. Then found the page again and turned down the corner.

He slept badly. Once it was his bladder, but the other times he simply woke, and each time the two crouched at the pool were in his head.

The light in the bedroom was grey. He dressed and went to the kitchen, performed his morning ritual of standing at the sink and drinking a glass of water. It was colder than yesterday, the grass lightly frosted, but with a clear and probably windless autumn day to come. He put on his sandshoes and walked to the workshop, the sand of the path crackling. The teapots and spouts were stiff enough to join, but with the stove not lit could safely be left till the afternoon.

Back in the kitchen he set the shopping pad on the table and jotted his own few needs, then drew a line and below it wrote *hard bread, tea, milk (long-life + tube condensed), Milo, honey, cereal* — he paused, put a question mark — *apples, cheese, meat (sausages/chops?)*. He read down the list. He had currying chops in the freezer, crossed off *meat*. Did children still drink Milo? Was it even still being made?

It was. But he chose the smallest. He took down then put back on the shelf Weet-Bix and from the other side of the aisle chose a toasted muesli in a strong resealable bag. Cans, too weighty, were deliberately not on the list, but he overruled himself and from the next aisle selected three different flavours of tuna in small ring-pulls. Coming back past the confectionery aisle he hesitated, then left the trolley and walked in and found Mars bars. They came in packs of four or six. He took a six-pack.

At the ford he brought his feet together on the last stone and checked the tiny beach for prints, hoping, despite the weight on his back — and which he would have to lug back *up* — that he might see three new sets, fresh that morning and leaving. The only prints were his own, from yesterday. He stepped onto them and walked to the rotting log and set the pack down, then returned to the ford and drank. The black pebbles in the water renewed the thought he'd had coming down the glen. How much of the creek they might have explored. He'd never bothered to hide the evidence of his rock-getting. The decomposed basalt he scooped up in his hands and the marks he left could, he supposed, to an urban mind, be mistaken for the digging of an animal. But even children couldn't read the shattered vein as natural. So if they had been up to the head of the creek they would know, and so would the man or woman, that the canyon had other visitors.

When he reached the rocks where he'd found the wrapper he halted. He'd heard them from here yesterday. There was just the low rush of the water leaving the pool. He was two hours earlier. But he continued to stand, staring up at the shrub he'd used as a screen. The silence didn't mean they weren't there. His own stillness was so convincing a pair of rosellas skimmed his head and crested the dam and dropped out of sight. A moment later he heard splashes and chirping. He rock-hopped to the pad etched into the earth to the left of the dam and climbed till the strip of gravel and the hump where they'd been squatting the day before came into sight. The rosellas were in the shallow where the hump entered the water. One gave a squawk of panic, and they launched into the air in a spray of droplets and clattered away upstream.

He stepped along the pebbles at the back of the beach. He badly wanted a coffee, but had left it too late. Air was moving up the creek, their sense of smell would be acute. At a dip, the pebbles both skittered and compacted, he found the start of a path he hadn't known was there, running up towards the cape. He halted and stared through the columns of trunks. It was like peering into the gloom of a cathedral. The path disappeared among mossed boulders and ferns and pepperbush and the five or six other species that made up the understorey, and which she'd have been

46

able to name but he no longer could. But as his eyes adjusted he saw between the trunks the pale yellow of unweathered sandstone. He brought the hanky from his pocket and quietly blew from his nostrils the fern spore he could feel tickling. He didn't want to be near that rock face and suddenly sneeze.

The path had not been made by the feet of children in a few days, it was old. They were just its latest users. The bucket had left traces, scrapes in the moss, flattened blades where they'd stood it to rest. A hair, made golden by a rod of sunlight, dangled from a leaf. He lifted it on his finger and it became merely white, but he saw the girl clearly. He released the hair into the air, moved again. He was watching his feet, but each time he brought them together on a boulder he returned his gaze to the rock face and watched for movement. From behind him came the soft slosh of the milk and a clank from the cans. The sounds had been with him all the way, but here were magnified. He debated whether to take the pack off. No, his breathing was louder.

He climbed for a further ten minutes, the trunks thinning and the pale yellow dominating the scape ahead. Suddenly, like yesterday, he heard their voices, and froze. He told himself they were further away than they sounded, because of the rock. Nonetheless he stayed where he was, debating again whether to take off the pack. What if he overbalanced in getting it off? Safer to leave it on. The voices came again, and again just children's. Was their adult not with them? Or just not talking? He was too far away to make out words, but could discern tone. They sounded happy. He hoped they were sitting — and facing one another. He didn't smell smoke. The girl spoke and the boy giggled, enabling him to get a proper fix on where they were. Some forty metres above him, and thirty degrees to the angle of the path.

He swayed his head to see through the leaves of the cissus clogging the lower branches of a clump of possumwood saplings and, like a lens shifting focus, made out one end of an overhang and its ceiling. It was this hollow space that was amplifying their voices. He could stay where he was and go on listening, wait for an adult voice. But what if they suddenly started down to the pool? He lowered his gaze and studied the path. It was twenty metres more of damp litter studded with mossed boulders to where the slope became loose rock with scattered ferns. He could try for a few more metres, even for the foot of the scree, but every step risked their hearing and bolting before he could say what he'd rehearsed.

He breathed deeply twice, trying to quell the fluttering in his stomach, then took a deeper breath and cupped his mouth with his hands. 'Hello? I'm a friend! My name's Russell! I've brought you some food!'

He heard a deeper female voice hiss 'Shit!' and the different hiss of nylon on itself, then a scuffle of feet, then silence.

Well, he'd answered the question, and his fear, of the parent being a man. It was the mother. There was no point calling again until she believed she'd got them to safety. He counted under his breath to twenty.

'I'm going to come up! All right? I'm by myself! As I said, I'm a friend! I saw the kids yesterday at the pool! My name, again, is Russell!'

What was almost a stairway was worn up the face of the scree. He climbed the last few metres in a crouch with his eyes trained on the rim, straightened when he thought he could see over, hoping he wouldn't meet the eyes of a scared but determined girl clutching a rock. He didn't, the shelter was deserted.

He stepped up onto the floor and thumbed off the straps and lowered the pack to the dirt. His scalp itched from tension. He took off the beanie and ran nails through his hair, then stood flexing his shoulders. Their escape route was plain, a slit between boulders that angled sharply up and disappeared. In the dust at its opening were fresh prints. He would have to enter the slit to see properly where it went, and that might send them fleeing higher. He turned and took in the shelter. It was some six metres deep and thirteen or fourteen long, canting up steeply at the rear wall and levelling to a roof a metre above his head. He half-expected to see painted animals or hand stencils, but the walls were bare, ferns and grasses growing in cracks stained black by seepage.

Lying at his feet, rucked from their flight, was an old tartan rug. They must have been sitting on it in the patch of broken sunshine hitting his boots. A large and very old circle of fire-scarred stones was set in the centre of the floor. Beside it, on a flat stone serving as a table, was the saucepan he knew and a larger one, a blackened steel-handled frying pan, plates and bowls of the heavy yellow plastic he remembered from picnics in his childhood, and, spread on a thin tea towel, an unmatched assortment of forks, knives, and spoons. He looked for a serious knife, but there was only the cutlery. He hoped a kitchen knife hadn't been snatched up and was now in a frightened hand.

The fire was dead, but sitting round and black in the ashes was an object it took him a moment to recognise, so long since he'd seen one, a cast-iron camp oven. It must already have been here, no child could have carried it. The cutlery looked to be of the same vintage, with thick tines and handles. Beside the slab table, its mouth covered by a second tea towel, stood the bucket, its handle still lashed to the carrying stick.

Between the fire circle and the back wall — for what reflected warmth there would be — lay three torn-edged planks of yellow foam rubber side by side on a sheet of clear plastic. The bags lay on the foam like worm casts, thin polyester things, not down. Two zippered sports bags he guessed held clothes. Hard on the arms to carry, especially a child's. Why didn't they have school rucksacks? Piled against the wall to the left of the foam planks was a stack of dry sticks. He looked for and couldn't see an axe, for proof had the broken ends of the bucket stick. 'Good!' he murmured.

So where did she store food? The only container he could see was a small plastic esky. *Listen, you're not here to sort out her living arrangements.*

He walked to the slit and crouched and studied the prints. The biggest set, he saw now, were heeled boots, not joggers, but weren't much bigger than the others. The kids were small, perhaps she was, too. 'Remember, though, she might have a knife.' He pushed himself up, knees cracking, and stepped into the opening of the slit and again cupped his hands around his mouth.

'Please, I'm no one you need to be scared of. I come up the creek to get rock for making pots. I'm a potter. I'm the one who breaks the stone further up, if you've seen it. Why you're here is none of my business. But I thought you could probably do with a bit more food. So I brought some. Okay?'

He was answered by silence, but thought it was a listening silence. He didn't want to say who he wasn't, it meant speaking the words 'welfare' and 'police'. Even if they could hear clearly, they were not words calculated to allay fear, might even exacerbate it. To someone a bit paranoid, to say what he wasn't might make him that thing. He could empty the pack onto the rug and go. But his curiosity wouldn't allow him to, he knew that. And a deeper worry. He'd seen now how rough they were living. They were candidates for pneumonia or breaking a leg.

'Look, I'm truly not here for any reason other than the kids and, if you don't mind, to get the rock I need. I've … been a parent myself and this can't be an easy place to be with young children. I thought you might need milk and bread.'

He debated whether it was better to remain straight or become cagey. Straight hadn't worked so far. 'I've brought some Mars bars, too. I found a wrapper on the path. I'm guessing the kids are fond of them.'

'We don't know you! Go away!'

The voice was not a woman's, yet not a child's. The ferocity, though, was maternal. He swivelled his head but the stone walls made it impossible to judge either direction or distance. Higher than where he stood was all he could say with certainty. And within hearing, which was what mattered.

'Well, if you'll let me, I'd like to make myself known. I'm Russell. What are your names?'

'We heard your name! Doesn't tell us who you are!'

'I'm what I said, I'm a potter. I make bowls and teapots. I've been coming to this creek for a long time to get rock for making glazes. I came yesterday and saw the children. Down at the pool. Floating the saucepan.'

He knew as soon as the words were out he'd made a mistake. She didn't reply. Instead there carried down to him muffled voices in what sounded like an argument, then the boy's, shrill and clear, 'No, *you* are! Bitch!' Whatever was going on, he had no role in it.

'You! Russell! Where do you live?'

The question threw him for a second. 'Where do I *live*? Um ... up near the old lookout.'

'What old lookout?'

'Well if you don't know it, it's a bit difficult to explain. I come on a track from the end of my road, down a glen. It comes out near where this creek joins another one. Then I walk up here. But up the other side.'

'But not from town, yeah?'

'Well, I'm on the edge of town. But I don't come on the track you probably used.'

'Why do you want our names?'

Again he was thrown by the veer in direction. 'Just … well, I don't have to. So we could talk using names, that was all.'

'What if we gave made-up ones. You wouldn't know.'

'That's true. I wouldn't.'

'Talk about what?'

'Do you mind if I ask first how old you are?'

There was a long silence.

'Why?'

'Well, there's just three sleeping bags here, and I don't think you're an adult, and I don't think I saw you yesterday, did I?'

He heard how garbled the reply was and issued himself a rebuke, *short and simple!* Again there was a silence. Then she said, 'How old are *you*?'

'Me? I'm seventy-two.'

'Your kids are grown up, ay.'

'My son died. When he was eight.'

It was like the bursting of a bubble in his chest, to be shouting the fact up a cliff to a stranger. There were people he'd known for years who assumed that he and Adele had been childless.

'I'm fifteen.' There was a pause. 'My name's Jade.'

'Pleased to meet you, Jade.'

He thought he might provoke, if she had any sense of the absurd, a titter of laughter. But all that sifted down the cliff was again silence. Then she called, 'Russell?'

'Yes?'

'You promise you're on your own?'

'I give you my word.'

'No! *Promise!*'

He did a doubletake, before understanding that the old oath so familiar it had rolled off his tongue without thought was not in her lexicon.

'I promise. No one else in the world except for you three knows I'm here.'

'You better not be bullshittin. If there's cops down there, or that DoCS cunt, you're in big trouble. We know where you live now and we know people who can hurt you if we tell em what you done.'

'If the police were with me, I don't think we'd be still having this conversation, they'd be up there.'

She gave a bark of laughter. 'Not them fat fuckin town cops.'

'Jade, I can't do any more shouting. The three of you make up your mind and let me know.'

He returned to where he'd left the pack and sat on a rock facing the slit and took his water bottle from the side pocket.

He listened for the rise and fall of their voices. Instead what reached him was the sudden slithering clatter of stones. A moment later the boy appeared in the slit. He was in the same trackpants and windcheater, but was bareheaded, the beanie clutched in his left hand, should he again have to run. His eyes flicked past Russell to take in the shelter, then he craned his neck in an attempt to look down the scree. He called over his left shoulder, 'Jade? It's just him!'

'Are you at the edge?'

The boy winced.

'Do what I fuckin said!'

The boy gave him a look, *stay there*. He stepped down onto the floor and, keeping him in sight, crabbed to the rim of the shelter. He threw a glance over the edge and skipped back to the slit.

'Jade? Can't see no one!'

Having done what he'd been sent to do, he could now stare. Russell was trying to puzzle out why she'd sent him. Was he expendable, under the least threat if taken into custody? He'd read that tribal people, at first contact, sent out their feeblest old woman to greet the strangers.

'Hello. What's your name?'

The boy's chin trembled from the effort of pressing his lips shut.

'You got in trouble, did you, for dropping the Mars wrapper?'

The boy gave a quick surly nod.

'Well, you can tell Jade it didn't matter, I was coming up past the pool anyway.'

He attempted a smile. The boy didn't return it. Russell noticed then how peeling and cracked the lips were. His own lips cracked in the cold, and he carried pawpaw ointment in the pack's front pouch, but vaguely remembered having taken it over to the workshop when he couldn't find the tube he kept there.

'I might have something you can put on your lips if they're sore. I'm not sure.' He waited. 'Do you want me to look?'

The boy gave no sign either way. Confused, but needing to move at least his arms, Russell began to reach to the pouch, but stopped when the boy shuffled backwards. He was trying to think of something reassuring to say when there came another clatter of stones, and the girl appeared behind the boy. She fixed her blue eyes on Russell's. There was no warmth in them. She, too, was in the same clothes as yesterday. Her hair was snagged in the collar of her windcheater and she flicked her head to free it, the gesture almost imperious. He remembered the self-possession she'd radiated at the pool. Keeping her eyes on Russell, she put a hand to the boy's upper arm and pushed him out of her way and stepped down onto the floor of the shelter.

'Hello.'

'Emma.'

He nodded. 'Hello, Emma.'

'She's comin.'

Had come, in fact, a teenage girl in a long brown dress almost mediaeval in its cut, with tight-fitting arms and flared cuffs. There was a costume shop in town, he'd seen such dresses in its window. He stood. The girl returned his nod, then swept the shelter and the scree with her own assessing gaze. Satisfied, she stepped down onto the dirt floor. 'Hi — Jade.'

He walked to her and offered his hand. 'Russell you know. My surname's Bass.' Her grip was swift and light, then she stepped in front of the boy and girl as if to say she'd made physical contact for them all. He retained the feel of her fingers, cool and damp, but the skin as roughened as his own.

'You don't look seventy-two.'

He shrugged. 'And I'd have put you at more than fifteen.' Her thanks, if that's what it was, was a twitch of the lips.

She was tall, looked almost level into his eyes. Hers were green. A silver ring disfigured her left nostril. Three smaller rings, also silver, frilled the gristle of her right ear. His eyes hadn't deceived him when he'd first looked at her, the blonde hair had streaks of pink. She was pretty, but in the pinched way of the boy and girl. Like their faces, hers too was all bones and planes, no flesh, not even around the mouth. To fine down faces to this, he knew, took longer than a few days of privation, it began at birth.

He turned and nodded towards the pack, then beyond it to the fire circle. 'Could we sit and perhaps make a cuppa? I've brought tea and milk.'

'We don't light a fire in the daytime. We got cordial.'

He mentally slapped himself. *Of course, cordial!*

'Cordial, then.'

She strode past him to the fire circle, her knees against the dress a loud whispering. The boy and girl scurried after her. He thought the dress might be velvet. It was a second skin to the waist, then fell in pleats to the tops of heavy black boots worn to white across the toes. Whatever it was, the fabric looked heavy enough to be warm, but he couldn't have said so with certainty. If they'd been born in the town they'd probably adapted to its autumns and winters. He had. But not, he knew, to the level of living in an open rock shelter. He lifted the pack and deposited it beside the slab that served as the kitchen bench.

She had set out plastic mugs on the stone. Not looking up from pouring the concentrate, she said, 'Tell him your names.'

'I done it,' the girl said. She jabbed the boy with her elbow.

'My name's Todd. T-o-d-d.'

'He can spell it, dumbo.'

'Em,' Jade said, 'get the rug.'

She dippered water from the bucket with the smaller saucepan and filled the mugs and handed him one. The girl returned with the rug and threw it to float in a perfect square to the dirt floor. She tapped him on the arm, pointed to a corner. Her right eyelid, he saw now, was swollen in the early stages of what he recognised as a sty.

The boy sat close to Jade, his hip against hers. She lifted her chin towards the pack. 'You said bread, yeah. We got nothin to put on it.'

'There's cheese and there's tin fish.' He dragged the pack to him, undid the flap and drawstring, then proffered the pack by the straps. She put down the mug and spread her knees and propped the pack between them. She drew out first the parcel of white paper, raised her eyebrows.

'Chops. They should still be frozen.'

She placed the parcel on the rug and tugged out by its twist the round-ended loaf, stared suspiciously at it. He guessed they'd only ever eaten white sliced.

'It's that kind so it wouldn't get squashed. You'll need a knife. The tins are at the bottom.'

She took out instead the block of cheese. It, too, needed a knife. She reached for a plate and placed it on the rug and lay the cheese unopened on it. She tapped the boy on the thigh and hooked her head. He stood and went to the mattresses. When he turned he was holding an eight-inch kitchen knife. Russell guessed he'd taken it from under whatever she used as a pillow.

She cut off the crust end and put it aside, made single-slice cheese sandwiches for the boy and girl. He declined, telling her the food was theirs. She made an open sandwich of the crust. The other two were already loudly chewing. He took the clickseal pouch from his jacket pocket and opened it in his lap and took out a date and some cashews, then dropped the pouch open in the centre of the rug and sat back and took a sip of his cordial. It was too diluted to identify with certainty, but he thought it was lime. The boy had stopped chewing. He leaned to Jade and whispered.

'He wants to know what they are.'

Russell looked at the boy. 'Which — the brown things? They're called dates. Try one. Watch out, though, they've got a seed in the middle.'

Despite the warning, the boy put the date whole in his mouth. Two chews and he stopped and pulled a face. When he lifted fingers to his mouth Jade slapped the hand down. 'It's in your gob, you eat it!'

She caught Russell's look.

'By now she's down Silverwater. Women's gaol. They got done for possession and dealin, her and his father. Just so you know.'

Not her father also, then. Or the girl's? It was too soon to ask about family history. 'When was this?'

Her eyes narrowed. She looked off into the trees. They were eating his food.

'We been here nine days. They got picked up in the Family — the pub?' He nodded. 'A guy there rung my sister soon's it happened, and she come round the house before the dogs showed up.'

'The dogs?'

'The DoCS arseholes.'

He noted the toning down of the language. Was it in deference to his age, he wondered, or his ignorance?

'And she's … where? Your sister.'

'Here — Katoomba. But she lives around, yeah. Then, but, she and her boyfriend were crashin in that old YMCA.' She saw his blank look. 'Near the high school?'

He couldn't bring up even the vaguest image of where she meant. He shook his head.

'They brung us down here. They knew it from when … She and him knew it, yeah — from before.'

'Yes, I'm asking too many questions. It's just you're talking about a side to Katoomba I don't know much about.'

'Why would you?'

'Oh, here — and Blackheath where I grew up — always had their —' he was about to say *dark side* — 'their underside —' wondered if that, too, would be heard as insulting, or at least judgmental. Well, it was out now, he'd said it. 'Just I don't think we had DoCS back then — doing what you're talking about — it was the police.'

'Fuckin still is.'

She spat the words, but past not at him. The boy and girl had stopped chewing and were watching his face. He reached down as calmly as he could and took a date, but his mind running in search of a different subject. It was beside him, the circle of stones, the camp oven.

'I think other people were living here well before your sister.'

She met his eyes again. 'Yeah. They got told it too. It's heaps old, she said.'

He nodded at the oven. 'And … do you use that?'

She began to reach to the lid handle, then drew back her hand. He was surprised to see that her throat and cheeks had coloured. 'We heat rocks in it. To put in our bags.'

'That's a smart idea. Yours, I'm guessing.' He loathed flattery, but told himself there were situations in which it could be just tolerated, this being one. He hurried on, though, rather than milk the moment. 'And for food, what — you go back up?'

'I don't leave these.' She hooked her head towards the kids. 'She and him come down. They have to watch, but. The cops know em.'

The younger girl had swivelled to look at the back wall. He followed her gaze and saw them too, a row of tally marks scratched into the stone. 'Five,' the girl said. *Emma*, he reminded himself.

'What's today?' Jade said.

'Saturday.'

'They come Monday. Why we're runnin out. Depends on her dole. If they're short they do a hit on a weekender. No shortage of them.'

It was a world he knew nothing of.

'How do you … contact her? There's no reception down here. You *do* have a phone?'

'Yeah. There's a bit if you climb. I'm savin charge, but.'

There was no point offering to charge it. She wouldn't leave the kids to collect it, and he wasn't coming down again with just a phone. He had his wallet, but it held at the most ten dollars, which was useless. The two young ones had been following the conversation, their eyes flicking to Jade when she spoke, but returning instantly to him for his answer. He realised what he was becoming, a hope, even perhaps a saviour. He needed a diversion. He nodded at the girl.

'Is that hurting — your eye?'

She touched the swelling gingerly with a fingertip and nodded.

'Rubbing it with gold's supposed to work.' He slipped off his wedding ring. It came easily now. 'Here.'

The girl looked instead to Jade. She shrugged. The girl took the ring and held it tentatively to the reddening on her lid.

'*Rub* he said!'

The girl bowed her head and began to move the ring.

'I don't know how long for. Maybe count to a hundred, eh.' The girl wanted the attention taken off her. He turned to Jade and lifted a finger towards the pack. 'The milk's long-life, but probably needs to go somewhere cool. I'd suggest with the chops.'

She emptied the pack, the dry goods onto the slab, the milk, cheese and chops into where he'd guessed, the small esky. Emma gave him back his ring, murmured thank you. When Jade made to open the front pocket he said no, the bulge was just an empty bag. That when he left them he was going up to the top of the creek to collect the rock he'd hiked down for yesterday. She came alert like a dog shown a stick. Could they come, she asked shyly, the second sign he'd been given that beneath the maternal fierceness was a teenage girl. 'We seen where you get it.' He *had* begun to wonder what they did all day. He doubted the zippered bags held any books. He'd deliberately not mentioned school, teachers perhaps in the same category as DoCS officers.

'If you want. It won't be very interesting though.'

The young ones led the way to a crossing higher up. On the other side of the creek was the pad his own feet had made and kept open. The two took off and soon vanished. He offered to Jade that she go, too, if she needed to keep an eye on them. 'No, they're right.' Once, pretending to follow a rosella, he glanced and caught her looking to their rear. Still not entirely sure about him, then. He quickly faced forward as her head began to turn.

They heard the young ones before they saw them. They were crouched each side of the green vein, Emma using a heavy ovoid pebble for a hammerstone, the boy picking up the slivers and piling them on a cushion of moss. He winced when he got closer. In violation of his deep respect for materials, the working face was white with shatter lines. How could they know? They were pleased with how much they'd already broken. He apologised for not having told them he wasn't taking this rock today, they were going further up. But he would take their pile the next time he came.

They hadn't explored beyond the vein of stone, believing this to be where the pad ended. But the boy and girl quickly found the break in the ferns and were gone again, not knowing where they were going, but possessed of too much energy to trail along at his pace. He and Jade found them a hundred metres on, at the foot of the cliff, standing bushed in the jumble of boulders roofed by tree ferns and struggling coachwoods. The girl opened her hands, *nothing here*. He lifted a finger towards the ledge over which the newborn creek ran after emerging from the cliff face.

Compared with bashing stone to splinters, the dyke was dull. He held open the leather ore bag while the young ones scooped up handfuls of the grey-black crumbs spilled onto the ledge and took turns to pour them in. Jade skirted the spill and walked to the face of the dyke and, with a stick, dug at the ancient lava. In less than a minute she'd hollowed out a small tunnel. She flicked the stick away and reached in and brought out a handful of the unweathered rock. She tilted her hand to the light and studied the clean glittering blackness, then grunted and spilled the crumbs at her feet. He sensed her assembling words.

'This's from an old volcano, yeah?'

'That's right,' he said not looking at her, but hearing he'd not quite kept the surprise from his voice. 'Very old, why it's crumbly.'

'We done volcanoes in science. Ig-something.'

'Igneous, you're spot on — volcanic rock. This particular rock's called basalt.'

'So …' she flicked her hand over the spill, 'how do you make rock into pots?'

He signalled to the young ones to stop scooping. Retaining the mouth of the bag in his hand he swivelled on his soles, but stayed on his haunches. *She lacks education*, he told himself, *not intelligence. Don't talk down to her.*

'Not pots, glaze — the shiny skin on the pots. Because it's been melted before, inside the volcano, when it's heated to a high enough temperature it'll melt again. And having lots of iron in it, that gives a black glaze. If I'm lucky, with streaks of dark blue or red, or sometimes little brown flecks that look like animal fur.'

'You sayin you heat it hot as a volcano.'

'No, no. But hot enough to turn it molten again, yes.'

He saw the word clearly in her face. *Bullshit.*

'I don't use it like you see it here — sorry, I should have explained. I mill it to powder, and I add ash from the fire and another powdered rock called feldspar to help it melt. But a pottery kiln gets very hot.' A scrunching made him look to his left. Bored, the boy was jabbing a dry fern rib into the loose scree. Emma struck the offending arm, and he stopped. She snatched the rib. Jade had kept her eyes on his face.

'Hot as an oxy?'

He wondered who the welder was. 'Not that hot. But thirteen hundred degrees centigrade — if you remember your two scales of temperature. That's not fireplace-hot, that's white-hot. A lot of metals melt at that temperature. The kiln has to be bricks.'

She frowned, and he saw his veracity being weighed again. Then she nodded.

'I think I seen a picture of one. In China or some place.'

'There's lots of them in China.'

'You been there?'

'I have, yes. To see them. My wife and I.'

He was startled on the return walk when a small hand took his. The boy didn't risk looking to his face for consent. He gripped back and shortened stride, coughing to swallow away the tightness in his throat. He couldn't, and finally had to pretend to sneeze so he could wipe his eyes. He thought he must have held a child's hand since Michael, but couldn't think whose child. When the path squeezed them into single file or became a scramble the boy reduced his hold to a single finger, but didn't let go.

At the pool he gently broke the tenacious grip. He took from the pack the small notebook he always carried and wrote his name and phone numbers and said if she needed help and couldn't reach her sister, and she had charge, to ring him. She glanced at the paper, then folded it and zipped it into the top pocket of her windcheater. He began, and stopped, the voice in his head warning that he risked being told it was none of his business. But he had to ask. Where was she planning to go? They couldn't *live* here. As he'd expected, she became evasive, said she didn't know, maybe Blacktown, to an aunt. Her sister was on it.

'Well, would you ring me? Just quickly, to say you're safe? And ... you've probably already thought about this — if one of you gets sick or hurt. It's a hard walk up from here. You might need help. Even … the police.'

'No way.'

'Well sometimes there's no choice.'

'That ain't!'

He backed off. 'Okay.'

He shook their hands, hers last, said he'd think of them next time he came up the creek.

'You will anyhow,' Emma said, 'cause we broke you that rock.'

'And I'll remember again when I put it on a pot.'

The smile she gave him was fleeting but pleased.

He looked back from the boulders where he'd found the wrapper, and they were still standing where the pad met the pool. He looked again when he reached the lip of the gully that would take him from sight, intending to wave. They were gone. It gave him an odd, perplexed feeling to know that this place he'd thought pristine was peopled, had been all along.

His own familiar kitchen felt odd after the 'kitchen' he'd not long ago left. He made grilled cheese on toast, sat at the table to eat rather than standing at the window. As he chewed he kneaded his right knee. There would come a day when it would require more than kneading. 'I'd better get a stockpile before then,' he said across the table, as if he and Adele were discussing their failing joints. Or pay someone younger to go down for him. It was hardly a 'secret' anymore.

He changed into work clothes and carried the ore bag over to the annexe. He poured half the rock into the heavy porcelain jar and added the balls and water, lidded it and lay it on its side on the rollers, and hit the switch to start the slow process of milling granules to slurry.

The teapots were ready. He pulled four handles and lay them on a batt to stiffen. The other four were having lugs and cane. He worked on each pot individually until it was completed, turning the foot and lid, then trimming the spout till it fitted the curve of the body, drilling the strainer holes and attaching it, and handle or lugs. He worked slowly and carefully, not wanting to overcut a spout or excessively thin a lid and have to throw a replacement.

By the time he lifted the last from the banding wheel and studied its profile, lowered it onto its batt, the windowless end of the workshop was in gloom. The dusty alarm clock said five. He'd managed to banish them from his mind as he worked, but now allowed them in. It was dark enough for a fire. She'd be frying the chops. Them and bread, he supposed, and an apple. And perhaps a half-mug of milk each. No, she'd save that for the muesli, give them cordial. He should have asked what else they had. But what was the point? He hung his apron and went out, rinsed his hands at the tank.

As he neared the steps he heard the distant rhythmic thudding of the drum kit. He stopped to listen. Again the insistent 4/4 which was all the boy seemed to know. He wondered would any of the three down there have ever played an instrument, and, too late to retract the thought, heard Adele's cross voice, *What are you talking about, they'd do music in school!* All right, owned then. They would never have owned an instrument. He certainly put in his hours with the sticks, Jerome. Younger than Jade, thirteen, fourteen. Anyway, still with a child's smooth cheeks and round face. And visibly fed. A language and their ages were about all Helen's two shared with the three. 'Well, insofar as they have a roof over their heads,' he said towards the drumming. 'But you're forgetting they're effectively fatherless.' How long had the man been gone? *Gideon.* Five years, it must be. Lucy would be struggling to remember him. He barely did himself. 'So not so different. Just more comfortable.'

How would the three visit their mother in gaol, and the boy his father, without attracting the attention of the authorities? She'd mentioned an aunt. He hadn't been able to judge then, couldn't now, whether the aunt was fiction. His damp hands were cold. He started towards the steps. Did he have kindling? Yes, the basket was nearly full. And the woodbox half. He raised his foot and thought, *omelette.* He stepped sideways to her herb bed, had to look hard before he made out the parsley.

He was stirring porridge when he heard an engine. He paused the spatula and listened. It sounded heavier than a lost car. He lay the spatula across the saucepan and ran to the lounge room windows and was in time to see pass the gap in the planted fence the back half of a white panel-sided Landcruiser and the word *RESCUE*. He ran back to the kitchen and turned off the gas, and out to the landing and pulled on his sandshoes.

He slowed when he neared the gap and glided to where he could see through the front line of wattles and not be seen. The cruiser was parked in shade, or in hiding, its nose into the casuarinas. Four men in white overalls tucked into high-laced boots were out and equipping themselves with belts and coils of rope. A metallic voice came from the open door of the cab but none paid it any attention. The tallest of the men adjusted the hang of the bandolier of rope he wore, then slammed the door and locked it. The other three were already walking towards the lookout.

When the four disappeared he sidled out onto the road. He could have spoken to them. But he hadn't trusted his ability to act the innocent householder. Why was he asking, he'd have seen in their eyes. They might then have asked *him*, had he seen three kids go past in the last week, kids he didn't recognise as local. No, better not to have given them any reason to be wondering about him on the way down. Let them believe they were wasting their time.

When he returned to the kitchen his eyes went first to the clock. They were younger, fitter. Forty minutes down, a slow couple of hours of checking the track for prints, maybe as far as Helga Falls, then back up, an hour. Around eleven, then, twelve maybe, depending on their thoroughness. That was another good reason not to have gone over to them. His boot prints were everywhere, and fresh. His belly went cold. There'd be prints at the ford going *towards* the rotted log, and coming *from* it! He clenched his hands, pressed them to his chin. 'Please! Read just that I sat there.' Even better would be if the lyrebirds had overnight turned all the tracks into a shambles. He stood for a moment in a dither. There was nothing he could do. He started towards the stove — and jumped when the phone rang! 'Be her,' he pleaded. Instead Helen Kent said, 'Russell, are you in the house?'

'Yes.'

'Did you see we've got police over at the lookout?'

'I did, yes. Rescue. I don't know why. I haven't heard anyone's gone missing. Have you?'

'No — that's what I was about to ask you.'

'We might find out when they come back up.' *But I very much hope not*, he added silently.

'You're … still coming over?'

He heard her trepidation that he might have changed his mind. Or even forgotten, the preoccupied 'artist'.

'If I'm still invited.'

'Of course you are! By then we might know. I'm not sure I've ever seen a police vehicle in the street.'

'Oh, in the past, yes. Not for some time.'

72

He'd planned to spend the morning throwing another run of bowls, but was too anxious. He worked instead in the annexe, where any and all sounds from the road would reach him. He resieved an ash and limestone glaze he wanted finer. He poured off the top water from yesterday's milling and tipped the slurry into a plaster bath to dry, then set the second batch to milling. At eleven, not trusting his ears, he walked out to the road. The cruiser was still there. Half an hour later he heard the squeal of a door hinge. He dropped the lid on a bucket and bolted for the gap in the planted fence, near its entrance forcing himself to slow to a walk. His heart, though, was threatening to burst through his chest. He crept to the last line of wattles. Just the four! None was speaking into a radio. The side panels were up, and they were stripping themselves of gear. One said something, and they all laughed. The mood was of men who'd done the job asked and now just wanted lunch and to put their feet up. He backed away till sure he was out of sight, then closed his eyes and stood breathing as she'd once shown him, in through the nostrils, hold, exhale through the mouth. He heard the motor start and doors slam. He stayed where he was until the grind of the heavy engine had faded to nothing.

Lucy opened the door to him. Her hair was freshly washed, and she wore jeans and an ironed yellow sloppy joe, printed on it a young man wearing an electric guitar. There was no name, the man evidently not requiring one to be recognised. He began to ask, thinking to display some interest in the girl's musical tastes, then realised just in time that all he would be displaying would be the abysmal ignorance of the old.

'Mum and me are here. Jerome's doing a sleepover.'

'Oh. I was going to compliment him on his drumming.'

He knelt and placed the small tissue-wrapped package on the carpet and began to unlace his right boot.

'You don't need to,' she said. 'We don't.'

'I know, it's habit.'

She shrugged. Despite the sloppy joe she radiated an adultness that brought to his mind the self-possession of Emma. She was, he was guessing, about the same age. But she was chubby-cheeked and clean, her eyelids flawless.

Helen met them at the kitchen doorway. She'd dressed, too, for the occasion, in a sleeved red floor-length gown with swirls of embroidery on the bodice. He searched for the word and, to his surprise, found it, 'caftan'. He'd not seen one in years, had believed them extinct. Two thoughts collided, where on earth had she found it, and that she tried too hard. He pushed both from his mind and held out the package. 'A little something.'

'Ohh! I said bring nothing!'

He saw her glance down and note his socked feet, bite her tongue. The girl was hovering, wanting both to escape and to see what the tissue contained. The kitchen table was set for three, an opened bottle of red at the centre.

'Friends' table,' she said.

He'd eaten here three or four times since Adele died and each time she'd said the same thing.

She rested the package on the cloth and peeled back the petals of paper to reveal the handleless cup, its temmoku a jewel-black against the tissue. The only fault was a halo on the side shielded from the flame, which was underfired, chalky. She turned to him with the cup cradled in her hands. 'It's beautiful.'

The girl pulled her hands down to where she could see.

'It's not for display, it's to use.'

She dipped her head. 'You have my word.'

He was instantly transported, shouting the same pledge up a cliff to a teenage girl who didn't understand and wouldn't accept it. He saw in the woman's light frown that his absence was visible. He willed a smile. 'For green tea, I'd suggest.'

Jade, though, was still in his mind. To speak of her without speaking of her he said, 'I don't know if you saw the police come back up. I just happened to be out the front. They didn't seem to have rescued anybody.'

'I'm sure it'll be in the dreaded *Gazette* if it was anything.' She swept the tissue from the cloth. 'Now, please — sit — dinner's nearly ready. Would you pour us a glass? Darling,' she said to the girl, 'there's juice in the fridge, you can help yourself.'

She'd remembered his partiality to merlot. They touched rims and sipped. Then she carried her glass to the island bench and whipped an apron from the towel rail and dropped its loop over her head.

He watched her. He didn't know her. Yes, he'd sat at his own
kitchen table five years ago while she sobbed and raged. But it
was with Adele that she'd made the transition from neighbour-
in-need to friend. He'd spoken to her weekly when she began
coming to the house for lessons. Adele had made a point of
bringing her over to the workshop to say hello and, if he was
throwing, to sit for a few minutes and watch. When, though,
she set up the studio under her house Adele more often went
over there, and weeks would pass without he and Helen seeing
one another. Adele had kept him informed as to what she was
working on, and on her progress, both emotional and artistic.
She'd asked if she could watch a firing, and he'd reluctantly
said yes. She'd come to two, the second time bringing Lucy.
He'd said nothing, but his demeanour had made plain that he
didn't welcome spectators, even discreet ones, and she'd been
sufficiently intelligent to read the signs even before he asked
Adele to have a word.

In the last eleven months he'd had to negotiate with her
directly. She'd returned manyfold the sympathy and practical
help she'd been given, taking turns with Hugh and Delys to
shop for him when he was incapable of leaving the house, and
persisting for weeks with soups and casseroles left at the back
door until he finally found the pride to ask her to stop. He
didn't know her age, but thought about forty. He had always
been sexually drawn to small slender women. Helen was neither,
would never have been. But she combined fine olive skin with

blonde hair and piercing blue eyes, and had the hands he admired in anyone, strong, and never still. The red caftan set off her skin and eyes. It hadn't been selected for that, he knew, but because it was 'arty'. She had put on a lot of weight when her husband left, then taken it off. Not to begin attracting men again, Adele had told him, but as a statement, the refusal to be a victim. She hadn't while Adele was alive gone out with a man, because that news would have reached him, but he didn't know if she had since. He didn't invite confidences and she didn't volunteer them. She had told him, though, that she was still refusing her husband the divorce his Thai 'fiancée' was insisting on. Not, she said, as payback for his not having paid a cent in maintenance, and not because of her Catholicism, but because he had never in the years he'd been gone even hinted that he missed the children. Only now was he making noises about 'could they fly over, he would pay', noises that had nothing to do with wanting to see them, and everything to do with her saying yes to the divorce.

'You're not drinking?'

'What?' He saw his hand on the table, fingers pressed to the glass as if in an arrested lift. He dropped his hand into his lap. 'I am, definitely, but I'm happy to wait.'

She'd taken from the oven a blue Le Creuset. She lifted the lid and steam ballooned into her face. 'Okay, the wait's over. Would you pop along to Lucy's door and knock and just call to her that it's dinner.'

The white balls on his plate proved to be potato dumplings. He'd never had them before and said so. Helen laughed, said neither had she, and thank you Jane Grigson that they'd worked! The casserole was beef, strongly flavoured with red wine. Reminded, he raised his glass, said they'd saved him from toast and scrambled egg yet again, and Lucy too laughed.

She no longer asked if it was too late in his day for coffee. They carried their mugs down to her studio, at the foot of the stairs walking into the smell of linseed oil, a smell he loved, and that took him back to his teaching days and passing the open door of the painting studio. He'd always slightly regretted that Adele had preferred watercolour. The room was rendered brick, in the day lit by two rectangular windows set lengthways high in one wall, and now by two reading lamps with strong white globes aimed at the ceiling. The room's original purpose had been a games room. The table tennis table he'd seen leaning against the wall the first time he'd come here, with Adele, was still here, but now with canvases piled against it. The canvas she obviously wanted him to see, though, was on the easel. He stopped to take it in from gallery distance, heard her halt behind him. It was, as he'd expected, a landscape — but the cliffs and chasms were gone! This was a landscape such as Vincent might have painted, a field of vivid green under a high blue sky, a dirt road and a red tractor for perspective, a distant backdrop of gums. The green was a crop, not wheat, though, or young sunflowers. He was about to ask when she said quietly, 'As you can see, my horizon finally allows for some sky.' She made a soft chuckle in which he heard no humour. 'Blue at that.'

'You painted it on the spot?'

'Here. From memory.' She moved to stand beside him. 'It's near Mudgee.'

'It's … barley?'

'Peas. I kept bumping up the green, but I'm still not sure it's right. But they were so green!'

'They are, Adele had them by the trellis-load. As you'd remember.'

'Yes. And on that note — and I so very much wish it had happened sooner, for the obvious reason — I've been offered a show. Not the black ones, these.'

'Oh, that's terrific! Where?'

'Here — Katoomba. Lost Bear. In December. He thinks they'll sell.'

'So do I.' He turned and put out his hand. They had never hugged. Not even her grief or his had brought them to that. 'It deserves to, it's a fine work.'

She'd blushed to the colour of her caftan. 'Thank you.'

'I think we need something a bit stronger than coffee. I've got a bottle of cognac over at the house that's been waiting for the right occasion.'

'I can save you the walk. Do you drink scotch?'

'Just the once, a very long time ago. Not since.'

'The day he rang I splurged on a bottle of Glenfiddich.'

*

He woke with a dry mouth. He turned onto his back, wincing at a jab behind his left eye. There was sun in the room. He'd overslept. He worked his tongue to make saliva and swallowed, thinking he must be getting a cold. Then he realised what it was — he was hungover! For a moment he was more amazed than ill. How had he drunk enough — and kept it down? 'It's spirits,' he whispered. *But so's brandy.* He closed his eyes. He didn't have an answer.

He walked very slowly to the bathroom, trying not to jar his head, and stood under the shower with the water pouring into and overflowing his mouth. He was gentle with the towel on his hair, but the headache, too, seemed to be abating. He was still amazed that at no time had he felt nauseous — not in her kitchen, not on the walk home, and not when he lay down. He wanted to tell someone. The person who came, weirdly, was Jade. 'For god's sake,' he said at the blur in the mirror.

He thought he remembered you needed something fried. He halved a tomato and fried the halves with bacon and two eggs. Then he made a full plunger of coffee. By the time he'd washed up and stood the few things in the drainer he felt almost as he did on any morning.

He threw the run of bowls the police had blocked. Just before four he heard a heavy motor and thought for a second they'd returned, then recognised the distinctive groan of its suspension as the wheels of the Hilux hit the sleepers bridging the roadside ditch and rolled onto the two-track that led to the splitting area and kiln shed. He didn't stop, Hugh would see the smoke. He was thinning the lip of the bowl he was on when he heard boots on the step and the door open. 'G'day,' he said at his fingers.

'And to you, good sir.'

The feet of the stool left the floor and were set down beside the wheel. Russell lifted his fingers from the bowl and leaned and studied its profile, then straightened and let the wheel slow. Hugh held in each hand a parcel wrapped in newsprint.

'What are they?'

'That new body.'

He stood one package between his feet and began unwrapping the other. Russell dabbled his fingers in the slurry bowl, wiped them on the strip of towel lying across his thigh. Hugh handed to him a white bowl, its overall salting light, but up one side a flare strongly pink at the foot and dying palely at the rim. 'They weren't lying, the bugger flashes! And very sweetly! Take a look at this.' He unwrapped and handed to Russell the second bowl, in his haste trapping the paper as well. He snatched it away, flicked it to the floor. The pink on the second bowl was even stronger, with an aureole of pearl grey. 'What do you reckon? Nearly up there with the original, eh.'

Russell moved his eyes back and forth between the bowls he held in the goblets he'd made of his fingers. Hugh couldn't throw a bad bowl and these two were lovely. He didn't say so, Hugh didn't care about the throws.

'Fired in the gas.'

'Yep. With a crucible each. Just touching the feet.'

Russell lowered his hands and grinned at him. 'Looks like I'll have to place an order after all.'

Hugh was reaching to take back the first bowl. He halted his hand, frowned. 'What order?'

'A dinner plate.'

Hugh laughed. 'Fuck, you're a spender!'

'Okay, a porridge bowl and a plate.'

'In that case —' he jabbed a finger — 'you can have the one in your hand.'

Russell shook his head, handed it back. 'Wrong shape and too small. A *hearty* bowl.' He became serious. 'When are you ringing them?'

'Soon's I get home. Wanted to show you first.'

'They twelve k blocks?'

'Yep.'

'Add two, will you, and I'll give you the dough. I'll try it under the guan.'

'Done.'

'You want a coffee?' He glanced at the dusty clock. 'Or have you reached your curfew?'

'A weak one.'

'Not here, the kitchen. I'm ready to knock off.'

He cut the bowl from the wheel-head and stood it on the crowded board, then drew a sheet of plastic over the remaining balls, tucked it.

At the house Hugh said his ritual words, 'Just go and say hello,' and headed in his socks to the bedroom, to the tea bowl. It had come to Russell from a man dead now twenty years, James Sedgwick, a collector of antique Chinese ceramics, and, enthusiastically, of Russell's modern interpretations. He had bought from every show. Both avoided openings, and it was some time before Russell finally met him, an arranged introduction at the gallery followed by an invitation to his house when Russell mentioned that he had seen Songs behind glass but had never held one. 'That can be mended,' the man had said. The house was a potters' Aladdin's cave. In its inner sanctum Russell was handed, one after another, seven tea bowls in oil spot or hare's fur, each nine hundred years old and each looking freshly lifted from the kiln. He'd almost dropped the last, certainly swiftly handed it back, when told casually the insured value of what he was holding.

He'd learned too late of the man's death to attend the funeral, but would have gone, deeply grateful for what he'd been granted that day. The day was returned to him four months after the funeral when a cubic-foot plywood box was delivered by special courier. Professionally wrapped and padded was the second of the hare's fur tea bowls he'd held, tucked down beside it an envelope of heavy cream paper. The handwritten note and accompanying certificate of provenance lay in the top drawer of his desk. He still took it out, not to read the words, which he had by heart, but simply to look at the signature in remembrance of the man.

To Russell

In honour of a true spiritual inheritor of the Song tradition, and with gratitude for the many hours of pleasure your pots have given me, this small token.

(And this necessary postscript, each of us, from opposite directions, being acutely cognisant of the fact that a pot is more than its aesthetic value. Should this one ever need to be sold on, its last valuation was $27,500.)

With my deepest regards
James Sedgwick

The bowl sat quietly on the bedroom dresser. No thief entering the house would have dreamed that it was, by far, the most valuable object there. Not wanting to scare himself, he'd never gone online for even a glimpse of its current value. Hugh, though, had, he was sure — could have told him in a flash if ever he wondered aloud. Russell called to him that coffee was up. He answered, but didn't immediately appear. A last fondling, Russell guessed. One of the pears piled in the fruit bowl had yellowed since morning. He took it to the cutting board and peeled and quartered it and carried the quarters back to the table and arranged them around the dates and almonds on the plate. Hugh appeared soundlessly in the doorway.

'It was a bit dusty, old son. I gave it a clean.'

'So do I.'

Hugh halted and lifted a hand, *hey, I was helping*.

Russell nodded down at the table, 'That one's weaker.'

Next evening he was standing at the open fridge trying to decide what to cook when he heard what sounded like a knock at the front door. No one who knew him came to the front. Someone lost, maybe. But he hadn't heard a car. He cocked his head and waited. The knock came again.

In the dim light of the forty they used in the hallway he thought for a second the girl was Jade.

'Hi. Russell?'

She managed simultaneously to hold his gaze and look past him. He knew who she was.

'Yes.'

'I'm Jade's sister.'

'I thought you might be.'

She had the same narrow, slightly feral face. Her blonde hair looked hacked with a knife. In the left nostril where Jade had a ring she had a small clear stone. He assumed glass, but, so small, it might equally have been a diamond. A black studded jacket hid her build, but her throat was as sinewy as her sister's, and the bulky sleeves probably hid the same thin arms.

'I'm Kayla.'

His eye was caught by a movement. A young man, also in black, was standing in the gap where he could observe both the house and the road.

'Okay if I come in?'

'Ah, certainly, yes.' He flattened himself against the door. She moved past him in a creak of leather and halted at the lounge room doorway and glanced in, then stood side-on and waited, her gaze flicking between him and the lit kitchen.

'And … your friend? What does he want to do?'

'He's good.'

He watched the figure as he closed the door. He didn't move. She was waiting. He motioned her along the hallway, but she shook her head, 'You go.' When she stepped into the kitchen her eyes went instantly to the other doorway. If you were a wallaby, he thought, your ears would be up and your nose twitching. Jade's words came to him, *they do weekenders.*

'I live on my own.'

She half-turned. 'She said you're married.'

'Was. My wife died eleven months ago.'

'Oh.'

The word conveyed no sympathy, was simply the logging of a fact.

'And she says you're a potter, yeah.'

He heard she'd never till now had need to speak the word. 'That's right. Not many of us about, no. Now, would you like a hot drink? I can do tea or coffee.'

'Nah.' She turned and faced him properly. 'If you're wonderin, we found you from the phone book. She give us your name.'

'Well, my description was a bit vague, so I figured something like that.'

'Um, you got juice?'

'No. Sorry. I can offer you a beer, though, if you'd like. Or wine.'

She shook her head. 'Tea, then.'

He thought as he turned towards the jug, *you're as short on the pleasantries as your sister*. But how many 'pleasantries' would they have heard growing up? He carried the jug to the sink, spoke with his hand on the tap. 'What about your friend? It must be a bit chilly standing out there.'

'He's good.'

He ran in water for one. He motioned to the table. 'Would you like to sit?'

'I'm good.' She folded her arms across her breasts, the jacket softly creaking. 'I better say why I come, ay.'

Another trip. Would she offer money? he wondered. He shrugged, 'There's no hurry. I don't get many visitors.' He switched on the jug and took the milk from the fridge, then went to the shelves to choose her a mug. He chose the better of his two early crawled shinos as a surface she would never before have encountered.

'She said you brung em stuff.'

'Well, I guessed food might be hard to get. She told you, I suppose — how I saw the kids.'

'Yeah. So I come to ask you somethin.'

'Please.'

She frowned. 'What?'

He was himself confused, then realised hers was again a profound unfamiliarity with pleasantries.

'I mean go ahead, ask.'

'Well … we was wonderin, me and her — like, could they come here, just for a bit, not long. Be safer. You know? You found em, so some other ba— … someone else's gonna.'

'*Here?* Aah … My goodness.' He dropped the bag into the mug and, for thinking time, looped its string around the handle. The jug had switched off. He spoke as he poured, glad that for a few seconds he didn't have to meet her gaze. 'I would think she told you also that I didn't just stumble on them. I go up that creek to get rock.'

'Yeah. But you seen the cave — Toddy and Em are too little, ay … for there. Me and him —' she hooked her head towards the road — 'we stayed there, but summer. And we was her age, Jade's.'

He placed the mug on the table, and a teaspoon, lifted the lid from the sugar bowl. She ignored the milk, spooned in two sugars, and retreated again to stand near the fridge, the mug in both hands. It, too, she'd ignored, it was just a mug. She took a quick sip, lowered her hands, her eyes not leaving his.

'Jade said you're old but not, yeah. You might be cool with it. Can't take em places we know, DoCS know em, too. Soon's me and him seen where your place is I thought yeah, go for it.' She took a longer sip, then, lowering the mug, lifted it again slightly and touched the rim. 'Thanks.'

'You're welcome. So … when you say "not long" … can you give me any clearer idea?' He heard now how she might interpret what he'd intended simply as a clarification. 'I mean when would you need an answer?'

They're children. Why are you hesitating? The girl was speaking. 'Pardon — what?'

'We was hopin tonight. Three, four days tops, yeah — for how long.'

'And where will they go after that?'

He saw her face close. 'I'm still lookin.'

'All right. Yes. Tell her they can come. I can invent a story.'

Her thanks was a terse nod. 'The little ones won't be no trouble, they do what she says, ay.'

'I saw, yes.'

'Did she say about our mother?'

It was a relenting of sorts.

'She told me she'd been arrested, her and Todd's father.'

'She rung me. I fuckin hung up!'

'From … gaol.'

'Dunno. Didn't give her time, ay.' She reached to the table with the mug.

'Might she be given bail? Because of … the littlies?' He was, he knew, speaking from a profound ignorance.

'Dealin? Wouldn't reckon. And who'd pay it? And DoCS'll be straight round sniffin her out! No way Toddy and Em are goin in care. Me and Jade been there! Bastards split us. Anyhow, there's no house, realos took it. They owed rent, yeah.'

'I see.'

Her eyes flashed — *see?* — the contempt quickly hidden. He felt his face prickle. He pointed towards the other doorway.

'Would you like to have a look? I've got a guest room and a study. Jade can use the study if she wants a bit of privacy and the littlies in the other.'

'Nah, they'll go in one.'

'Well, you might still take a look, eh. So you can at least give *them* some idea.'

She followed, he thought to humour him. He switched on the light and stepped aside to allow her to enter. She stopped in the doorway. 'Yeah, here's good. She and Em can go in the double and Toddy on the floor.'

'You don't want to look at the study?'

'Nah, in here's good.' She stepped away, waited for him to turn off the light. They walked back to the kitchen. Time, he sensed, was up. Too long in a strange house or she wanted to join the young man. Or did she simply have what she wanted? Whatever it was, her manner had changed.

'So — tomorrow okay? To bring em?'

'Oh, that soon? Ah — all right. But do you have any idea what time? It's just I'll need to do some shopping.'

'About same as now? I can ring you.'

'Yes, that'd be good. I'd suggest an hour before. I very rarely have visitors, but you never know. I wasn't expecting you, for example.'

He'd hoped for a flicker of smile at least, but was given nothing, deepening what he'd begun to suspect, that she was without humour. But why should she find humour in any of this?

He walked her to the front door. He hesitated before offering his hand, not sure she'd respond. She did, but her grip, like her sister's, quick and weightless. The young man turned his face towards them when the door opened, but stayed where he was. Russell didn't ask how they'd got here.

He closed the door and went into the dark lounge room and stood where he could look through the window and the white of his face not be seen. She'd joined the young man in the gap. They stood face to face and close, talking. Then he threw an arm across her shoulder and they walked towards the road. He scampered to the bedroom, to the window bay, and a minute later saw them emerge from behind the living fence, a bulky darkness moving not on the easier walking of the bitumen, but on the ill-defined track that did for a footpath and which ran along the shadow-line of the trees.

He returned to the kitchen and sat at the table. The only real possibility of an unannounced visitor was Helen Kent. Hugh had been yesterday, would be back Thursday night. He and

Delys he would have to tell the truth, ask them to stay away from the house till they'd gone. 'They'll think you're mad.' He grinned. 'Well you are. The cops are after them.' He couldn't, though, repress another grin. Now that he'd agreed, he was excited. It was only for a few days, no one but him would see them. They'd have to stay inside. That might be difficult, especially for the boy.

He needed to decide in advance what to tell Helen, in case she or one of her two got a glimpse of them. Hugh and Delys wouldn't be silly about Jade. Helen, he couldn't say, even if he told her the truth. A fifteen-year-old girl, dependent on him to hide her and her brother and sister. He could threaten her with turning the little ones over. He thought of Helen moving about in her kitchen. She was essentially a stranger. Probably he was traducing her, but he would feel safer with a story. The most innocent and logical identity to give them was relatives. Not grandchildren, obviously — she knew about Michael. A niece's, then? His non-existent sister's youngest daughter. And from where? 'Don't get too clever. Sydney somewhere, even a suburb down there they might already know.' Jade had mentioned Blacktown, where the real or fictional aunt lived. She wouldn't have just plucked the name from the air. Blacktown, then. It didn't matter that he'd never been there himself except from a train window. Why would one visit a niece? But her children might visit *him*, their semi-grandfather up in the Mountains. It wasn't school holidays, though. *That* he'd have to think through, find something plausible.

His hand strayed to the shino mug. She'd drunk only half. How old was she? If Jade was fifteen. Seventeen? Like Jade she looked older than she probably was. Neither was a girl, they'd left girlhood behind, they were women. He stood and walked to the sink and poured out the tea and rinsed the mug, inverted it in the drainer. He was hungry! Of course, when she knocked he'd been standing at the fridge. He was sick of eggs. He pulled out the dairy tray and found the stick of kangaroo salami Hugh had insisted he try. Roo pasta, then. With garlic and parmesan.

After dinner he stripped the guest room double bed and draped its doona over the back of the lounge. He was getting miles ahead of himself, but knew he wouldn't be able to watch television or read. He went into her study, to the divan, and rolled its thin mattress and lugged it into the guest room and leaned it in the corner. Moving around had raised dust and a mustiness. He couldn't face vacuuming at night, that was too much. He opened a window and closed the door so cold air wouldn't seep through the whole house.

There were books, and there had been board games. He remembered ludo and Chinese checkers. He had no idea where she might have put them, or even if they'd been kept. He looked in the logical place, the built-in press in his study. The room had been Michael's. There were no mysterious cartons. They would have to settle for books, then. He wasn't sure anymore what was there. He wheeled the chair to the low bookshelf standing by itself. Prominent in the top row was the illustrated *Treasure Island* he'd been given by his own parents. Michael hadn't wanted the story, complaining that the words were too old. They had, though, looked at the captioned plates, he explaining who Jim Hawkins and Long John Silver were in an effort to enthuse him. Russell slid the book out but didn't open to the beginning, knowing what would happen, he would read the first sentence and be hooked. He opened instead to the first plate, then wished he hadn't, having forgotten what it was, the roadway outside the inn, Blind Pew with his bony fingers in a vice grip on Jim's shoulder and nose in the air like a dog. Russell stared at the boy's terrified face.

They wouldn't arrive till night but his mind couldn't settle to the work, too full of the conversations he needed to have, firstly with Hugh and Delys and then with Helen. The only sensible thing to do was to have them. He covered the bowls, closed down the heater and walked back to the house.

He changed his clothes and pocketed his wallet, then returned to the kitchen and sat with pad and pen. The list grew to a page. He was startled. He retracted the pen and sat trying to think when had been the last time a child or children had stayed in the house. Visited, yes, John Farley and his sparky twins, already making pots, on their way through from Mudgee some four months ago. But stayed, slept? Years. He couldn't think who they would even have been. Not family. Adele had been an only child. His brother had never married. It bothered him that his mind was a blank. He stood and peeled the sheet from the pad and folded it, pushed it into the pocket with his wallet, and went into the pantry to fetch shopping bags, taking down from the hook his usual two and two more.

He was in Coles nearly an hour, searching up and down aisles he never entered. He rang from the old Civic carpark. Hugh answered. They were both at home.

It was a cool enough morning that most everything could stay in the car, but not the ice cream. He'd had the foresight to ask the girl to put it in a separate plastic bag. It was only when he lifted the bag from the zipped insulated bag that he realised how thin its plastic was, the tub's label visible. If they hadn't heard the car he could slip into the kitchen and get to the freezer before he halloed. But when he rounded the corner of the house he saw both of them through the windows, Hugh at the sink. Hugh lifted his hand from the tap and gave him a wave. No escape, then. By all means, Delys would say, move things around if there isn't room. But since when was he buying ice cream? And they'd be straight into what he'd come for. Well, so be it. He wasn't going to be apologetic.

She was seated at the bench with her knife, peeling an orange. She glanced a smile and looked back down. Hugh it was who said, 'Sure,' adding when the door sucked shut, 'You having guests?'

'Yes. To stay, actually. Which might get a bit tricky. So what I'm here to ask is — could we give tomorrow night a miss, please.'

Hugh turned from the machine, Delys lowered the orange. Russell pointed to the row of cups. 'Maybe do the brews, and we'll sit out on the deck.'

Delys interrupted only once, to enquire whether 'they' had a surname. It was such an obvious question he was dumbfounded that it hadn't occurred to him. He hadn't, he said — till Kayla — needed to know, and she'd left him with a lot more to think about than surnames. Anyway, from the bit of history he'd gleaned, they were quite likely all three different.

When he was leaving Delys hugged him, then looked hard into his eyes. 'Be careful, please. I'm not saying the sense you've formed of her and the sister is wrong. Just … careful.'

Hugh walked him out to the car. He waited till Russell was behind the wheel, then leaned to the open window. 'That goes double, eh — what Del said.'

Russell quelled a surge of irritation, but not entirely, as he heard when he began to speak. 'Look, I really don't think I'm being played for some sort of mug, Hugh. I think it's genuine they don't have anywhere else to go. Not immediately.'

'Okay.' He took a step back. Then he bent again to where he could see Russell's face. 'Have you … given some thought to where they're going to be all day? I mean, are you planning to be in the workshop, leave them in the house?'

'God's sake, there's nothing there to steal, you know that as well as I do. So yes, I'm going over the workshop! I might even suggest they come too, give them some clay. Just need to keep them out of sight coming and going.'

Hugh pursed his lips, nodded. 'Ring if there's a problem, eh.'

He started the engine. 'Watch your feet.'

'I am, might need them to kick you with.'

Russell grinned. Hugh didn't.

If Helen had ever told him which days she worked, he'd forgotten. No, he was flattering himself, he never properly listened. He glanced up her driveway as he passed. No car, but equally it might be in the garage.

He put away the shopping. The freezer had never looked so full. He walked automatically to the grinder, then reminded himself he'd just come from a coffee. 'So have another one!'

When it was poured he brought the handpiece to the table and sat. The lying would dry his mouth. After three rings the machine cut in. 'Hallelujah,' he breathed and waited for her voice to finish.

He told her not to worry if she saw children in the yard, they weren't trespassers, he was minding his niece's three, up from Sydney. They had a few days' dispensation from school while their parents flew to Perth to move their father's mother out of her house and into a nursing home. They'd been here before, and he'd lined up plenty for them to do. He would pop over for a cuppa when they'd gone and see how the work was progressing, but trusted it was going well. He ended the call, then almost hit redial, worried that he hadn't been plain enough. But surely she would take the hint.

He changed into work clothes and went to the annexe. After a search he found under a pile of folded sacks the second of the two blocks of Walkers red earthenware he'd bought years ago to demonstrate to a weekend class the relative properties of earthenware and stoneware. The plastic, he was delighted to see, was still intact, just one corner chewed. The clay, when pressed, took his thumb. He lifted the block onto the wedging table and removed its twist, then stood it upright and peeled down the plastic and took up the cutting wire.

He quartered it and wedged and balled the quarters, then found a bucket with a lid to keep the balls moist. It would be perfect to hand-build with, dogs or dolphins, pinch pots. Hopefully, they wouldn't want them fired. Or he could do a small bonfiring with them. That, though — the glow of a fire with kids around it — might attract Helen's two. 'Leave it at the modelling.' He dropped the balls into the bucket, hesitated with the lid. He'd forgotten the feel and smell of a fine-grained earthenware. He lifted the top ball back onto the table and cut slices and made three bowl-size balls. He dropped the cut clay into the bucket and lidded it, then carried the balls into the workshop and sat at the wheel.

For old times' sake he threw three of Seth Bligh's 'oatmeal' bowls, with their high sides and strong heavy bases thrown down to the foot. Seth hadn't believed in wasting time on turning. Cut the base level next day, and give it a foot ring, and that was all the finishing a bowl got. He leaned away and studied the three standing side by side, mirrors of one another. Fifty-plus years and he hadn't lost the form. He heard the man's voice, *those're keepers, lad.* Except they weren't, because they wouldn't ever be fired. He slapped the bowls together into a brutal lump, which he carried back to the annexe and dropped in the bucket.

The rest of the afternoon he filled with 'drudge', making up fresh wadding, cleaning props, barrowing wood from the stacks to the kiln shed. At five he returned to the house and lit the heater. Then he made up the double bed and the mattress on the floor, fetching an extra blanket for both and leaving it folded on each doona.

When it was dark he walked out and stood in the middle of the road. Curtains glowed at the Kents', blue smoke curled from their flue. The air was cold enough that he hoped not only them but all the neighbours were in for the night. Kayla hadn't said how they might arrive. It was quite possibly on foot — and lugging conspicuous bags and bundles. He asked himself again, should he have offered to go in the car to wherever they proposed to come up from the valley? It wasn't too late, he could ask when she rang. But he heard what she'd say. *We're good.* And they almost certainly were, or would be. So standing out here looking up the empty street was achieving little. The phone might even *be* ringing. He was a fool, he'd forgotten even to leave it on message! He spun and broke into a jog.

The phone was silent. He fed the heater, washed his hands, separated sausages and filled the griller tray. Then he scrubbed and diced potatoes and set the steamer over an unlit burner. He took down the big-bellied ash-glazed pitcher they'd used for barbecues and poured in a long measure of lime cordial, added ice cubes and tank water, and stood the pitcher on a mat in the centre of the table. Then he made a simple salad of lettuce, tomato and cucumber, without dressing.

His fingers were lifting from setting the bowl on the table when he heard a car. There'd been no call. He listened for the slew of gravel which would tell him the driver was lost and making a circle. What reached him was the low continuing throb of its motor. A door opened and slammed, another. He darted to the stove and sparked the burner under the potatoes, then ran to the lounge room windows and opened a slit in the curtains. The back half of the car, dark blue or green, not a taxi, was visible in the gap. They were standing at the roadside sorting out and shouldering bags. The car slid away, the driver giving the horn a soft *bip*.

He turned on the hall light, but left the porch light off. Jade came first, carrying a bulging sports bag and a rolled sleeping bag tied with a belt. She nodded to him, then backed against the wall to hurry the young ones past. The girl and boy carried their rolled and tied sleeping bags, and Emma a pair of grubby yellow rubber boots. Kayla came at the tail with the other sports bag. The young ones stopped dead in the hallway, causing a jam. 'Move!' Jade commanded and they took two steps and propped again, staring towards the lit doorway. It was, he realised, a fortnight since they'd last been in a house, let alone a strange one.

'That's the kitchen,' he said, unsure of what tone to use to overcome their shyness. 'You hungry?' They looked down, nodded. The girl's eyelid was still inflamed. 'Well leave your things here and go through, eh.'

Still unable to look at him, they bent at the knees and deposited the sleeping bags and boots on the carpet, then stood with backs pressed to the wall as if they'd not heard the second part of the instruction. Kayla had closed the door. He knew better than to ask about the young man. Jade dumped the heavy bag against the wall and dropped the sleeping bag on top and blew a relieved gust of breath. He opened his hand in readiness but hers stayed at her side. 'Thanks for this.'

'You're very welcome. I feel better about you being here than down there.' He smiled, not sure but hoping she had more humour than her sister. 'You made me feel a bit guilty about being in a warm bed.'

Her grin was quick and nervy. 'Yeah, well you weren't supposed to come there.'

'I was, but not when I did.' He pointed along the hallway. 'I've started dinner, come through and I'll put the rest on, then I'll show you where you'll be sleeping.'

Kayla had paid the kitchen no mind the first time, and didn't now. The little ones, though, took two steps inside and stopped, their mouths falling open, heads slowly swivelling. He was on his way to the stove but halted — what was the matter? — then realised that from the height of a child they were looking up at cliffs of pots on every side, row above row of mugs and teapots, stacks of bowls, plates, and platters, and on every benchtop, and crowding every flat surface, even the top of the fridge, spice caddies, storage jars, and crocks. Jade's inspection, he saw, was more discreet but no less amazed. He ducked his head, weirdly embarrassed, and went to the stove and sparked the griller, heard the soft whoosh. She said as he turned, 'Did you … make all these?'

'Not all, but a lot of them, yes.' The embarrassment was in his voice. 'I have been a potter for a long time.'

'Was she one too? Your wife.'

'She sometimes had a go at decorating them.' He pointed to a platter with sun orchids leaning in the deep windowsill. 'That's one she painted. But no, she worked at the botanical gardens at Mount Tomah. You might have gone there for science.'

She shook her head.

'I did,' Kayla said, surprising him. She'd not spoken since arriving.

'Do you remember seeing the orchids? They were her specialty.'

She shrugged. 'I just remember goin.'

Jade flashed her a look, *you could at least lie,* and the return look, *why?* He said quickly, 'She was retired by the time you'd have gone there.' He pointed towards the other doorway. 'Okay, everything's on, so let me show you where the bathroom is and your room and you can take your things in.'

He narrowed the table spacings and set a place for Kayla. He tested a sausage with a knifepoint, remembering that Michael had insisted they be well done. They were, and he turned the griller off and mashed the potato, sprinkling in chopped chives, but leaving out his customary lemon pepper. He put the bowl and the platter of sausages on the table and cracked the seal on the bottle of tomato sauce, then went to the doorway and called them to the kitchen.

Kayla didn't sit, asked for a second plate. He fetched one down and went to the drawer for an additional knife and fork. She filled the two plates, heavy on sausages and bread and light on salad, and asked if he had a torch. He took the small one from the everything drawer, tested it, handed it to her. She slid it and the cutlery into her left jacket pocket and lifted one plate in her right hand and balanced the other expertly on her forearm and went down the hallway. *You've done waitressing then as well as weekenders,* he said silently to her back.

It was a meal without conversation, but their table manners were better than he'd expected. The little ones, though, ate more than he thought possible, the girl, Emma, clearing her plate in the time it took him to eat one sausage and half his mash. She crossed her knife and fork hopefully and tried to catch Jade's eye without catching his. 'Yes, you can have seconds,' he said. 'Serve yourself.'

'And me?' the boy said.

'Of course.'

'You ain't finished,' Jade snapped. 'You're eatin the lettuce or no sausage.'

The boy looked at Russell, then down at his plate when Russell arched his eyebrows, *she's your boss, not me.*

He heard the front door push open, and Kayla came in. They, too, had hoovered the food. She thanked him and carried the plates and cutlery over to the sink. He asked did they want dessert.

'Nah.'

She hooked her head at Jade, who rose and followed her outside. The boy and girl shot nervous glances towards the hallway until Jade came back in. She closed the door. She sat again. 'She'll ring you in a couple of days.'

'Me?'

'You answerin's cool. Better if my phone stays off.'

She helped herself to more salad, but no more sausages. When their plates were empty a second time Russell made to stand and was told no. She nodded at the two. The boy gathered up the cutlery, Emma stacked the plates and carried them to the sink. They returned for the bowls and platter and Jade said, 'One at a time — and two hands!'

He'd stewed pears. He asked whether they wanted them, or just ice cream. The boy looked at her, got a nod, said, 'Just ice cream please.'

He jumped up when they'd emptied their bowls, said it was their first night in the house and he would wash up. He saw her gaze flick towards the sink. 'We've never had one,' he said. 'She thought them a waste of water.'

'So ... how long's it been ... you know, just you?'

His throat tightened. He'd expected the question at some point, but not phrased so directly.

'I thought Kayla might have told you.'

'No. Only that she ... died.'

'Eleven months.'

'Was she sick?'

Emma, he saw, was listening, eyes fixed on his face. The boy was staring vaguely at the woodcut of banksias on the wall above the phone.

'No, it was sudden. She had a stroke.'

'My daddy's dead,' the girl whispered.

He thought he'd misheard and looked at Jade, who confirmed with a lift of her brows. His impulse was to kneel and take the girl in his arms, but that was impossible. He had, though, to do something with the welling-up in him. He put out his hand, and she lifted hers to be taken. He squeezed the fingers gently, controlled the urge to put out his other hand and stroke her hair. He released her hand, looked again at Jade.

'Was this ... recent?'

'She was three. She don't remember him.'

'I do!' the girl said.

'You don't,' Jade said flatly. 'You remember his photo.' She waved a finger above the two. 'Can they have a bath?'

'What? Yes, of course. Please, you don't need to ask about things like that. For as long as you're here it's your house. That goes for food, the radio, books. Okay?'

'Thanks.'

The boy beckoned urgently to her, *come down*. She bent for him to whisper in her ear, and straightened, suppressing a grin. 'He wants to know if you got only a radio, no telly.'

Russell laughed, but stopped when he saw the betrayal that crossed the boy's face. 'Sorry. Yes, mate, there's a telly. In the lounge room.' He traced the other hallway in the air with his hand. 'Along there and across from your door.' He turned again to Jade. 'Just one thing I'd like to clarify, if you don't mind. You *are* ... all brother and sister?'

'Yeah. Kayla and me are same dad. Toddy's she got on with before her and Em's split. I pissed off, was livin with my old man down Wollongong, but he's a prick, and his girlfriend didn't want me there, so I come back. Had to anyway, she went back usin, and they were dealin it, heaps, and weed, Jarrod and her — Toddy's old man. From the house and round the pubs. No way known they weren't gonna get done.'

He was about to mutter *I see*, then remembered in time the

look of contempt Kayla had flashed him.

'Kayla said your mum tried ringing her. She must at least be a bit worried about you.'

'Yeah, now she can't get nothin! Other reason I'm leavin my phone off.' He saw her gaze go inward, then return, a decision made. 'I dunno what you know about smackheads.' She pointed. 'How them two even got fed — when her and him were out of it I'd rat their wallets and ring a cab to Coles, yeah. I'd get Em to school, but some days I'd have to stay with Toddy — if she'd shot up. One time they drove down Melbourne, just took off. I had to do a house so's we fuckin ate! Now she's "worried". Well bad luck. She won't be hearin from me.' She spun, hooked her arm. 'Come on you two — bath.'

They heard the whip in her voice and vanished through the doorway.

'Jade?'

She halted, looked at him.

'I bought some ointment for her eye. It's a little tube, in your room. It says wash the eye first with a warm flannel, okay, then squeeze some in.'

She nodded. 'Thanks.'

He washed up, absently dunking plates, bowls, while his mind expanded on the glimpses given him of their world. Went *back* using, she'd said, which explained Kayla's bitter remark about her and Jade being taken and separated. So how old had they been? The age of these current two? And how often did it happen? 'Went back' didn't necessarily mean only twice, there was probably a whole history of getting off then using again. He snorted softly. 'You're a junkie expert now, are you?' He should certainly *not* be proffering glib guesses about the woman's state of mind! There came the clunk in the pipes as the shower was turned off, and he heard then the gurgle of the emptying bath. He snapped back to what he was doing, grabbed up the cutlery and ran it under the hot tap, dumped it in the drainer, peeled off the gloves.

They returned to the kitchen with clean shining hair, and in different if not entirely clean clothes. The filthy windcheaters had, he was glad to see, stayed in their bags. The morning would be time enough to point them to the laundry. And to school them in the story he'd invented for Helen. They wouldn't need telling to stay out of sight. Emma's eyelid shone greasy. He asked if it felt better, and she nodded. The boy asked could they watch telly. Of course, he said, and that he would come, too, in a short while. He didn't want to reveal on their first night that the pantry held Mars bars, that seemed too much. He badly needed a coffee, though. He should offer something. Who, he asked, wanted a mug of hot chocolate?

When he carried in the tray some ten minutes later they were watching young men and women swinging on vines and crawling through mud, to what end he didn't know. He pretended an interest by asking a few questions, which they answered without taking their eyes from the screen. When he stood with his empty mug he saw the girl's eyes follow. He went to his bedroom and fetched the borrowed book he'd finally started, a biography of the eccentric Japanese potter and gourmet Rosanjin. John Farley had sent a slightly testy email. He carried the book out to the kitchen and closed the door and sat at the table. He'd read only a page when the door quietly opened. It was her, Emma.

'Hello. Are you after something?'

She shook her head. She pointed back over her shoulder. 'What's that game?'

Thinking she meant the survivalists, he was about to say she should ask Jade when he realised what she really meant. 'On the little table — in the window bay?' She nodded. 'That's called chess.'

'She said checkers.'

'She's nearly right. The board looks the same.'

The girl hovered.

'You want me to show you?'

She looked at the book open between his hands. He closed it and stood.

He turned on the playing lamp and sat and nodded her to the seat opposite, his hands already moving the pieces swiftly back to their starting squares.

In forty minutes she had memorised the names of all the pieces and how they moved, and could execute three of his standard openings. He cleared clutter from the board and set up a trap to take her bishop with his knight, using a pawn as bait, and asked what her move should be. She stared for a few seconds then moved the bishop to safety. He set up another, threatening her queen with both rooks, one of them five squares away, and she evaded that, too. He set up a third, this against himself, telling her she could take his queen with her knight, not this move but the next. She moved wrongly, saw in time, and jumped the knight to where it threatened both king and queen. 'Yes!' he burst out. 'Good girl! I *have* to move him, and you've got her.' The excitement in his voice brought Jade from the lounge room.

'It's called chess,' Emma said, not lifting her eyes from the board, 'not checkers.'

'And,' he said, 'she's got the brain for it.'

'You tell him why?' Jade said down at the girl. She didn't wait for an answer. 'When she's home she's playin computer games nonstop.'

'*So?*'

'So just tellin him. That you're not some genius.'

He didn't state what he believed, that nothing prepared one for chess but chess. What interested him more was the flash of jealousy.

The boy was asleep on the couch. He offered to carry him. Jade scooped him up as if he hadn't spoken. Rebuffed, he returned to the kitchen and closed the door and sat again at the table and opened the book. The door opened to Emma come to say goodnight. He didn't want to inflame jealousies further and said nothing about tomorrow having a proper game. He'd read only a further page, was thinking of bed himself, when the door opened again. Jade came in and closed the door behind her. He saw she wanted to talk. He shut the book on the tooled leather gumleaf, which had come inside Adele's last-ever present to him, *The Hare with Amber Eyes*. He motioned to the chair opposite but she shook her head. 'Only be a minute, we're already stoppin you doin stuff.' He began to say not at all, and she spoke over him. 'Kayla's sayin don't tell you nothin, yeah, but I said we're stayin in your house so you need to know what's goin on. She's tryin to find our mum's cousin — down Sydney. One time we went to her. Other times to our gran, but she's died. Anyhow she's moved, mum's cousin, and we dunno where. We left word, yeah, we're lookin for her. Kayla's hopin a couple of days. Anyway, that's so you know.'

'Thank you. But you're not putting me out. As I said, I'm glad you're here rather than down in that cave. And I need to tell *you* a couple of things, if you don't mind staying a bit longer than your minute.'

She nodded but went on standing at the closed door.

'Firstly, though, let's talk about security. I suspect you're ahead of me, so what have you told them, the littlies?'

She was well ahead of him, had instructed them that a knock on the door or a voice other than his and they were to run silently to their room and get under the bed and stay there until she or he called to them that it was safe to come out. He didn't say what he thought, that it sounded rather melodramatic. Good, he told her. But it might not always be possible to avoid a visitor, so they all needed a story. He'd given his friends Hugh and Delys the truth because Hugh would have been coming to the house the following night to play chess and they were not people he lied to. The only other person who might just arrive was the woman across the road or one of her children. To her he'd given a story about who they were. He told her the story, and that she should rehearse the littlies in it, especially Todd, till they could repeat it. 'What parts of Sydney do you know? You mentioned Blacktown.'

'That was bullshit. Our gran was Marrickville.'

'Fine. Let's use Marrickville.'

Anyone else who arrived unexpectedly they should act shy and leave the talking to him. Although if he needed to introduce them he would use their real names, it was too hard to remember made-up ones. But, he told her, he didn't think any of what he'd just said would be necessary. A week often went by without anyone calling to the house. There was no reason for the next week to be any different. 'All the same, I don't think it's a good idea for them to go exploring like they did down there.'

She gave an impatient toss of the head, 'I already told em.'

He pushed back his chair. 'We've gone well over your minute. You're sure you won't sit, I'll put the jug on?'

'Nah, she won't be asleep, she'll be waitin.' Her mouth flickered in a smile. 'They asked me what they're supposed to call you. It's "Russell", right?'

'Goodness me. Yes! Please.'

'And ... she seen that photo. In the hall? That's your son, right?'

'Yes.'

'She asked me what's his name.'

'Michael. And my wife's was Adele.'

'Yeah, I seen it on that picture. In our room.'

He nodded. *Of course.* It would be one of the first things a stranger's eyes went to. She'd chosen one of her best for the guest room.

'Tomorrow I'll need to do some work, but we can talk about it in the morning. I get up early, so I mightn't be in the house. If I'm not, come over to the workshop.' He pointed at the window. 'The building over there. You'll see smoke coming from the chimney.' He dipped his head. 'Goodnight. I hope you'll be warmer than last night.'

'Already. Heaps. Kayl and me were gettin worried about Toddy.'

'I don't blame you,' he said carefully. In the few days since he'd last seen the boy the eye sockets were hollower, the cheekbones more prominent. 'He certainly filled up tonight, though, they both did.'

The voice reached out from the guest room, 'Jade?', the beginning of panic in its rising inflexion. She spun and snatched the door open, 'Comin!'

A bit before seven he came past their closed door and imagined them asleep in an unaccustomed snugness, nothing of each head visible but the hair.

They were in the kitchen, the little ones at the table with glasses of milk and eating white-bread toast and honey, Jade standing at the trembling jug, a mug on the bench with the tag of a teabag hanging over its side. They said hello, gave him shy smiles. He hid his surprise and returned the greetings, suppressing the urge to know why they were up so early and asking only whether they'd had a good sleep. Already, though, he was wondering about the rhythmic clicking coming from the landing, the laundry. Jade saw the direction of his eyes. 'That's zippers. I put your machine on. I hope that's all right.'

'You beat me, I was going to suggest it.'

The boy came and stood at the stove with his toast and watched him make porridge. He didn't know its name. Russell asked did he want a small bowl to try and he wrinkled his nose.

He told them he was going to his workshop, he had pots he needed to finish. They could come too, if they wanted, he would give them clay to make something. The boy turned on Jade an anguished look.

'He was wantin to watch *Pokémon*.'

'On the television?'

'Yeah.'

'Well, he can if he wants.'

She turned to the boy. 'You're here on your own, but, right. Em and me are goin with Russell.'

When twenty minutes later they started along the path the boy trudged in their wake.

He set a fire, gave the boy the matches. He'd cheered up by the time they closed the door on bright flames. Russell sponged clean a space on the benchtop and set out batts to build on and a selection of gravers and old bamboo turning tools, then carried in from the annexe the bucket of balled earthenware and dumped a ball on the bench. Jade had stood with folded arms observing the preparations. When he turned to her, arched his eyebrows, she said she didn't want to make anything. If he didn't mind she wanted to watch him work. He didn't mind, he said. It was just that what he'd be doing might not be very interesting, he wasn't throwing fresh pots, he was finishing some bottles. It didn't matter, she said. He pointed to the stool, then to a spot by the wheel.

He got the two started, tearing off a chunk of clay and quickly fashioning his party-piece, a smiling owl. They grinned and clapped, then went silent, calculating, he saw, how to emulate and surpass. They hadn't ever built with clay, but had used playdough. A legacy of the creek perhaps, they weren't finicky about getting their fingers sticky. They clawed from the ball the raw makings and announced what the lump was going to be, Todd's a predictable dog, Emma's a crocodile.

He unwrapped the bottle chuck of hard unfired clay from its plastic and stood it on the wheel-head, then set the wheel turning and centred the chuck with gentle pressure from index fingers and thumbs. He stopped the wheel and made a rough coil of the lump he'd lifted from the scraps bin and, as he thumbed it around the base of the thick flared cylinder, began to talk her through what he was doing and why, speaking not at her but at the clay under his thumbs. A bottle couldn't be stood on its neck, to turn the foot you needed to stand it upside down inside the chuck, its shoulders gripped by the chuck's rim and another, thinner, coil he'd make in a minute. She'd snagged on 'turn', asked what it meant. He had the same thought as at the dyke, *don't speak down to her*. 'It's cutting the excess clay from the base, bringing the curve you want right down to the foot. Then you cut a circle, or at least a depression, out of the centre so it'll stand. A flat base is rarely dead flat, or it bulges in the firing, and you've got a pot that rocks.' He looked at her, saw the information go in.

He had forgotten the intensity children were capable of. The two worked in a trance of concentration broken only by a delighted giggle or the occasional grunt of annoyance. Each time he slid from the saddle to return a bottle to the racks, fetch the next, he paused to allow them to show him what they'd done, describe what they intended. Only once, after a series of increasingly cross sighs, did the boy come to the wheel and stand waiting. Russell dropped a shaving in the tray and let the wheel slow. 'What's the matter?'

'His tail keeps fallin off.'

Russell lifted his foot from the kick-bar, put down the tool. 'That's a common problem. I'll show you the answer.'

He sat on the stool, and, their heads now level, the boy leaned into him, his chin on Russell's shoulder, breath warm on his neck. Russell quelled the impulse to draw him onto his lap. The price of keeping him clamped to his side was restricted movement of his left elbow, which he gladly accepted. He fashioned a stumpy prop, then reattached the torn tail and instructed the boy to hold it up while he slid the prop under. 'There. That's all we do. Then later we take it away.'

The boy stood straight, removed his breath. 'Thanks.'

Jade had the same intensity, watching like a hungry magpie and weaving her head when the movement of his arm obscured the tool. It was several times on the tip of his tongue to ask about school, using the pretext of whether she'd done art and hadn't that included pottery. There was only the one government high school, down near Echo Point. It must be where she had gone. What, he wondered, happened to truants these days? She would certainly know. The last two weeks wasn't the first truancy for any of them. She broke her silence and into his thoughts with a question far from his.

'Where's all this clay come from? Not what they're usin, the red stuff. That the bottles and all those —' she gestured towards the racks —'are made from.'

'Well, the same as I go and get rock for glaze, I dig up clay. At Shipley. From an empty dam on what used to be an apple orchard. I've been going there for a very long time. It's now a horse paddock.'

'How far is it?'

He stared at her. 'What — Shipley? It's up here, the Mountains. Out from Blackheath.'

'Oh. We stay just round Katoomba.'

He almost, again, muttered the fatal words *I see.*

'One day, though, I'll likely have to do like most potters and buy clay in bags, get it delivered.' He smiled. 'Or maybe dig a lot now while I still can.'

She didn't return the smile, studied him as if he were slightly thick. 'You pay someone. Town's full of dole kids.'

The words were almost Adele's. He said, 'It's crossed my mind,' and, to end a conversation that had veered unexpectedly into the personal, peeled away the coil holding the bottle in the chuck and lifted and turned the bottle right side up, thumbed off a smear, and slipped from the saddle to carry it to the racks.

At just after eleven — longer than he'd thought they'd last — the boy and girl said they were hungry. Jade stood, said she'd do them something. First, though, they wanted him to inspect what they'd made. The boy had two dogs, more generic quadrupeds than recognisably dogs, but each with a successful tail, and a little thumbed-out bowl for water. The girl's crocodile had grown in proportion to the skills and confidence she'd acquired as she worked, and was a brute, the scales incised with the curved tip of the old nib-holder he'd given them, and, her pièce de résistance — not there when he'd last come by — the jaws clamped on a human figure waving its arms and legs. She was smirking with pleasure at the look of horror he knew was expected of him. 'My goodness. Whoever *they* are, they're in big trouble.'

'And they deserve it,' she said with relish. She spared him the need to respond by jumping to her feet and asking breezily, venom gone, 'How long to it goes hard?'

'Oh — properly hard, about three days.'

'Okay.'

She broke the bow at her waist and ducked her head through the loop, dumped the oversized apron on the stool.

It was both a relief and oddly lonely not to have their presence behind him, and the small noises — the squeak of the stools, the soft clack of bamboo being picked up and put down, squirts of laughter. An hour passed. He hadn't expected the two would come back, but had hoped Jade might. He turned the last bottle and carried it to the racks, halted at the bench on his way back, his gaze again caught by the figure in the crocodile's jaws. She'd given it neither clothes nor hair, it was impossible to tell whether the figure was male or female.

119

Along the croc's side she'd scratched her name in bold capitals. He ran a finger along the letters to remove the frills of drying clay. The other three bore the 'modern' names parents copied from magazines and television. Who had chosen 'Emma'? The dead father?

She'd hung out the clothes. Washing had brightened the windcheaters, but removed little of their engrained filth. When he came into the kitchen he heard the television. Three washed plates and three glasses were stacked neatly in the dish rack. He made a cheese and pickle sandwich and took it back to the workshop.

He returned at five, the yard in dusk. The television was still on, cartoon voices drifting into the kitchen. He didn't disturb them. He got trackpants and a clean tee-shirt from the bedroom, and his house jumper, and had a shower. Then he cooked one of his standards, bolognese sauce and spaghetti. The smell lured the three out. Curiosity satisfied, the young ones returned to their cartoons, but Jade stayed, asked for a job. He'd already set the block of parmesan and the grater on the cutting board, to do when he had a moment. 'You can grate some of that for me. About half.'

She studied the grater then tentatively gripped the handle. 'Up and down, yeah?'

'That's it.'

'This that same stuff like in a shaker?'

'Yes, but a fair bit fresher.'

He didn't get the grin he'd angled for. She gave him a grave nod and glanced at her fingers. 'Back in a minute.'

He heard her return, but deliberately didn't watch her. But the sound was right. She stopped twice to show him how much, and, when told enough, swept the pile with the blade of her hand into the dish he'd set out, and laid on top, after surreptitiously studying it, the carved ebony spoon. She asked which plates she should get. Bowls, he told her, and pointed to the ash-glazed ones on the lowest shelf. 'Four of those, but not the chipped one.'

They'd eaten other pastas — 'them tubes', the boy told him — but had tackled only tinned spaghetti. He demonstrated how to twirl a fork and in seconds they had it. Again he was struck by their fierce natural intelligence. After emptying her bowl for the second time Emma leaned to her sister and whispered. Jade lifted a finger, *ask him yourself.*

'Can I have bread, Russell? For wipin?'

'Of course you can, we all will — me too.'

Jade washed, Emma dried, he put away, the girl telling him what she was going to make tomorrow, a house, and wanting to know if he had 'one of them things', miming its use.

'A rolling pin.'

'Yep!'

Jade and the boy returned to the lounge room and the television. Emma hovered in the hallway. He nodded, and she dived into 'her' seat, shoving its cushion aside. He set up the board with all its pieces, giving her white. A few minutes into the game Jade appeared carrying the cane armchair, a thick book under her arm. She placed the chair at right angles to the board and opened the book on her lap — he glanced, *The Reptiles of Australia* — lifting her head to watch when he explained a move and turning pages when her sister's pondering dragged on. It was a lot of instruction to take in and after an hour the girl was flagging. He suggested they leave the pieces where they were and continue tomorrow night. Jade had closed the book on her finger and was studying the board. 'Unless you'd like a go?'

She shook her head. 'No. But in the mornin can I have a go at makin a pot? Not with fingers, spinnin one.'

'Throwing. We can certainly have a go. It's just I've never tried teaching anyone on a kickwheel. The places I taught had electric wheels.'

She stared at him. 'You got electricity.'

'Yes. But the man I started with didn't. I used to say it's like preferring to stay on your old pushbike even after you can afford a motorbike.'

She laughed. He saw for the first time a gap where the cutting teeth met the molars. She promptly shut her mouth.

He asked her to help get the young ones started. She sat with the boy, who, inspired by his sister's crocodile, wanted a triceratops. Russell fetched the marble slab and sat with the girl, showing her how to hammer out a ball with her fist then use the rolling pin to work it into a sheet. She would need six, he told her, four walls and the roof. He gave her the rolling pin, told her he would come back when the sheet was flat and even and they would cut the wall. Now, though, it was Jade's turn.

He sat her at the wheel without clay, told her she was spending ten minutes just using the kick-bar till she got the feel of it, could speed up and slow down. She gave him the look she must have given teachers who chose to waste her time. He shrugged. 'I can't turn the wheel and at the same time guide your hands. Not unless you'd like to sit on my lap.' He got the response he wanted, she laughed, but controlling her top lip.

He knelt and positioned her foot on the bar, then gripped her ankle and gave her the rhythm, keeping her foot firmly planted until the head was spinning, then slowing the action, telling her the flywheel would now do the work, but she needed to give the bar a push when the head began to slow. He stood and watched. At this, too, she was a fast learner. He patted her shoulder. 'Good, you've nearly got it.' He pointed at the clock. 'Ten minutes, speeding up, slowing down, up again. And smooth, yes, not jerky.' He had, he heard, fallen as smoothly into his old teaching voice.

He worked with the young ones, his back deliberately to the wheel, but his ears tuned to the rise and fall of its hum. At the end of the ten minutes the boy had a barrel on legs, the girl a wall with pre-cut windows. He told them it was Jade's turn again. He went out to the annexe and made up eight half-kilo balls. He displaced her at the wheel and, talking her through what he was doing, threw three simple cylinders. Was she ready to try? She nodded. They threw two wonky ones, she giving no sign of discomfort at his hands on hers. On the third he took his hands away, and she continued the throw, finishing with a cylinder that pleased her with its height, but not its wavy rim. He congratulated her, told her to set the wheel-head spinning again, and took up the corked needle and cut the rim level. Then shocked her by tearing from the new rim a thumb-sized chunk. With the shock still in her face he told her to set the wheel going and passed her the needle.

She threw two more cylinders unaided. He deflated her again by telling her she was keeping none of the three and showed her why, the fat walls. He squashed his three into one another, then, avoiding her eyes, made her do the same with hers. He slapped the sculpture into a lump which he took to the other end of the table from the kids and re-wedged. He made eight new balls, delivered them to the wheel and left her to it, reminding her only to keep slurrying her hands.

The boy was dejected, had given up on his dinosaur. That was okay, Russell said, he'd show him how to make coils and build a pot. The lure of the new was too much for the girl and she abandoned her half-made house, wanting to make pots too. In minutes the two were in near-hysterics at the worms and snakes that, instead of his neat coils, rolled out from under their palms.

He blundered to his feet, telling them he needed to go to the toilet. Once outside, he stumbled to the back of the glaze kiln and stood staring blindly at the brickwork of its chimney until his turmoil subsided to a level where he thought he could sit again between their merry laughters.

At twelve they stopped for lunch. She had kept two of her attempts. Was that all right, she asked. Yes, he said, clay was re-useable until fired. But tomorrow the better ones she'd make would change her mind about these two. She scowled. He knew what at, the 'tomorrow'. He apologised, but after lunch he needed to be on the wheel. She was welcome to watch if she wished, or she could do what the little ones had been doing, coil and build. She turned away, said over her shoulder it didn't interest her. The two were following the exchange, the boy puzzled, the girl worried.

'There's only one wheel, Jade.'

'Do I look like I'm blind.'

Emma caught his eye, gave an almost-imperceptible shake of the head, startling but also silencing him.

In the kitchen she emerged from her sulk enough to ask did he have pottery books.

'One or two, yes.'

He ushered her into his study and left her gaping at the wall of spines.

They didn't return with him to the workshop. He fed the fire, then covered her cylinders and their half-made hand-builds with plastic and took his hat from the peg by the door. He did a walking meditation to the cliff edge and back. They weren't removed entirely from his mind, but shrank to a distant corner. He wedged and balled the buff clay from the base of the dam wall and threw ten large blossom jars. They, too, he covered with plastic.

All three were, like yesterday, watching cartoons. He showered, then baked gemfish fillets and, following the instructions on the packet, the frozen potato wedges he'd bought for the photograph of happy children tucking in. When they came to the table she apologised. He glanced at Emma. Her eyes stayed aimed at her plate, but the smug mouth gave her away.

After the washing up he and the girl sat in the window seats to continue the suspended game. They'd been sitting only a couple of minutes when the front door opened and closed. The girl said without lifting her gaze from the board, 'It's only Jade.'

'It's dark, where's she going!'

He'd spoken before realising the trespass. He couldn't retract without sounding foolish. The girl gave him a courteous out, placing her index fingertip on the head of a pawn as if conflicted and asking her own, but deliberately foolish, question, 'How many again can I move him from here?'

You're her sanctuary, not her keeper, he told himself. *And don't pester this one.* He lowered his weight again to the bench's hard padding.

'Have a think.'

'Oh — yeah! Dummy me.'

She had not returned an hour later when he halted the game and made hot chocolate. But when he carried a mug in to the boy he heard the door and a moment later she was standing in the lounge room, cheeks burnished by cold.

'Hi.'

'You look a bit nippy. Would you like a hot chocolate?'

'Yes please.'

She actually appeared pleased, her eyes were alight, her mouth had lost its customary tightness. When he continued to look at her she gave a small shake of the head and crossed to the couch and sat beside the boy, whose eyes had not left the screen.

When he and the girl resumed the game, Jade carried out the armchair, then went back and fetched the book she'd chosen to peruse while watching them play. His heart threatened to choke him when he saw what it was, *Chinese Glazes*. He fought down the urge to snatch it from her, turn to the Song bowls, lay it back in her lap. She would eventually reach them. The suspense, though, made it difficult to give his full attention to the game and the girl's questions.

He didn't insult her by allowing her to beat him. When he told her the game was over, he'd won, she gave him a serious stare, then, for what seemed fully a minute, roamed the board with her eyes. At the end of it she nodded as if to say, *yes, I'm satisfied you're telling the truth*, and asked could they have another game. Yes, he said. But first he needed to talk to Jade about the book she was reading. She looked up. He asked had she seen any pots she liked. A few, she said. But she was looking more at the photos of guys throwing. And at the kilns. She tilted the page. 'They're like your long one, but they're big as caves, they got people standin in em.'

'Well that's what they're called in Japan, cave kilns, ana-gama — and here. We've borrowed their word. But the Chinese invented them. Mine's on a much smaller scale, yes, I have to crawl in to pack it. But the principle's the same, a sloping tunnel with a fire at the lower end and a chimney at the other and the pots in the middle.' There was no need to tell her that his would never again know a fire. 'I have another book in there just about the kilns. If you want.'

'Nah, this's heaps.'

'It certainly is. One I still look at often.'

'You went there, ay — you said. Down when we was gettin rock.'

'Adele and I, yes.' He nodded towards the page she had open. 'To look at those. Especially the ones where some very famous black tea bowls were fired. There's photos of the bowls further on.'

'That where you got the idea?'

'The inspiration, let's say. But I use Shipley clay and Megalong rock, so I finish up with Blue Mountains pots.'

'But ... so what? That's cool.'

128

'I agree. It's not a complaint.' He thought to say, *in fact, it's a philosophy.* That would divert them from what he wanted to say next. 'Not now, but tomorrow, I'll show you a bowl I have in my bedroom. It's better to see it in daylight.'

'From China?'

'Yes.'

'How did you bring it?'

The girl had been sitting with folded hands and half-listening. Now she groaned softly and reached fingers and thumb to a pawn and began spinning it on its square.

'Tomorrow. Someone's getting bored.'

After breakfast he took her into the lounge room and told her to sit. He brought the bowl, asked her to open her hands in her lap and placed the bowl in the bowl of her palms. He sat beside her.

'This came from one of those kilns. Don't get nervous when I tell you how old it is. Nine hundred years.' She raised her eyes to his, in them something like horror. 'It's all right, you can't drop it, just hold it like you are.' He directed her eyes back down. 'This streaking is called hare's fur. You know what a hare is.'

'Like a rabbit.'

'The black and the brown are both iron. The iron in mine comes from that basalt we collected, but this probably came from using an iron clay for both glaze and body.'

She glanced at him, looked back down at the bowl. 'Was it … expensive?'

'For the man who bought it. I was given it.'

He was not quite finished explaining when she interrupted softly, 'Can you take it.'

He lifted it from her, gripped the foot in the fingertips of one hand and raised it to the level of their eyes. 'See the curve — how relaxed yet how strong it is? The man who threw this probably threw a hundred a day.' He lowered the bowl into both hands and stood. 'It lives in the bedroom. By all means go in and look at it, but I'd ask that you don't pick it up.'

The young ones were finishing a noisy breakfast. They didn't want to come to the workshop, the boy wanting to watch cartoons, the girl to learn moves.

Before bed he'd fetched from his study the primer that had been Michael's and his own travellers' set in its scratched and stained leather case and had shown the girl how to 'read' and transfer a move from the page to the board. She'd been slow to grasp the concept, but more, he thought, from a difficulty with reading itself. She had, though, fallen instantly in love with the miniature pieces, exhaling thrilled disbelief when shown that the feet were magnetised. The leather case lay now on the table beside a splash of milk. He said nothing. It had lain on many and dirtier tables.

He demonstrated to Jade how to knead, then left her and lit a fire in the workshop. When he returned to the annexe she was leaning on the table, chest heaving, face red. 'Yes, it's hard work.' He slapped the clay back into a loaf. 'Watch again. It doesn't come from your arms, you use your weight.'

They made up ten balls. He oversaw her centring of the first on the wheel-head and returned to the annexe. He didn't want her trying to wheedle an opinion after every throw.

She wasn't afraid to cull. When he went back in she'd used nine of the balls but had only two cylinders and a crude bottle sitting on the ware board. One of the cylinders was almost passable. He asked her what she really thought of the bottle after seeing those in the books. She silently lifted it and dropped it onto the other failures in the recycling bucket. She slid from the saddle, asked would he throw a bottle with the remaining ball. He motioned her back on, telling her that her guess was right, a bottle started with a cylinder. She threw the new cylinder, but pushed too hard when she began to open the belly and split the wall. She peeled the half-thing from the wheel-head and dropped it in the bucket. When she slid again from the saddle he nodded at the two on the ware board and told her to take the board over to the racks. She gave him a level stare. The side of her nose and its ring were streaked with dried slurry where she must have sneezed or brushed at a fly. 'For now, all right.'

She smeared her hands down the apron and picked up the board. He watched her carry it to the racks, stand for a moment deciding where. What a swift odd turn his life had taken.

A teenage girl with a ring in her nose was sliding ware into his drying racks.

That night Kayla rang. They were on dessert, warmed packet apple pie and ice cream. He handed the phone to Jade. She didn't, as he expected, carry it into the hallway. The conversation was short, at her end mainly yes and no. She stood the phone in the charger, returned to her seat. She spoke as if he wasn't there.

'Greg got picked up. They didn't have nothin so they had to let him go. But she's still freakin, ay.'

'Where?'

'The Y. She reckons they're watchin the place. She and him are crashin at Flynnies.'

The language shut him out, he was an eavesdropper in his own kitchen.

Emma pulled a sour face.

'Yeah, I fuckin know. But where, ay?'

The girl lowered her eyes, spoke at the bowl. 'She found her?'

Jade acknowledged his presence for the first time, a flick of the eyes and away.

'Reb's on it, he's ringin her back tomorrow.'

'Reb. Sure.'

'Well who else, smart-arse!'

Without warning, the boy began to cry. Russell looked at Jade. She nodded. He turned his chair, tugged on the boy's sleeve, 'Come here.' The boy stood and walked into his arms, buried his face in his shoulder.

*

Next morning the upper at the toe of Emma's left jogger finally parted company with the sole. All she had were the yellow rubber boots. He offered to take her into town and buy her new joggers.

It was the first time he'd seen Jade indecisive. She acknowledged that Emma couldn't go everywhere in rubber boots. At the same time she didn't want her in Big W. He should take her old joggers and buy something the same. He'd already seen the girl's face at the prospect of new shoes. He wanted her to have a pair she chose, not he. They didn't have to use Big W, he said. He would take her to the shoe store. The couple there knew him, there'd probably be no other customers, he could say she was his niece's daughter and there'd be no fuss.

It proved to be as simple as he'd said. The wife measured her foot, laid out a range on the carpet. She walked up and down in two pairs, red then purple, chose the purple. He blinked when told the price, forty-nine dollars. For two small shoes. 'They'll last,' the woman said. 'She'll grow out of them first.' When the woman reached to unlace them he said no, she'd wear them home. He didn't register what he'd said until the girl looked at him.

With them on she would no longer come into the dust and clay of the workshop, would not even cross the threshold. On the afternoon of her second day of ownership she was seated in the slat chair outside the door with the travelling set and primer open on a clean ware board laid across the arms. Every few minutes she would call him out to pronounce a word. He had brought buckets and sieve into the workshop to be near both the boy hand-building on the table and Jade on the wheel, and was making up a fresh batch of guan to use on the teapots. Each time the girl called him out her eyes went first to his coated hands, fearful that the creamy liquid might drip onto her joggers. Whenever the boy wanted her to look at what he'd made he had to carry it to where she sat. So when she burst through the doorway all three of them jumped, he nearly tipping the bucket.

'A woman and kid are comin!'

He grabbed a towel for his hands and hurried outside. The visitor could only be Helen with one of her two. She didn't need to come to the workshop, he would head her off. But they were already at the back of the kiln shed. He dropped the towel on the arm of the chair the girl had vacated. Helen waved.

'We won't disturb you, we just thought we'd pop over for a sec with an invitation.' She was looking past him at the workshop doorway. 'I think we gave your visitor a fright.'

'Ah … yes — she was engrossed in one of my chess books.'

'Oh! Bit more than the level of game we're offering.' She placed an arm around Lucy's shoulders and drew her in front of her. 'Lucy was wondering if they might like to come over. Rather short notice today, but maybe after school tomorrow.'

He forced a smile. 'Well … I suppose only one way to find out.' He stepped aside, ushered them past.

Jade had completed her throw, was letting the wheel slow. She smiled at Helen, 'Hi — Jade,' displayed her slurried hand, *sorry*. 'That's all right, I can see you're all busy,' Helen said. 'I'm Helen, from across the road, and this's Lucy.' Emma was seated at the far end of the bench. When Lucy stepped clear of her mother she stared, then dipped her head, had to be tapped on the shoulder before she mumbled 'hi'. Emma had cowled her face with her hands and was staring down at the primer. He wondered was this some weird ritual shyness between girls of this age. The boy, though, was looking at them openly, nodding when Jade introduced him.

Helen moved to the table and Lucy grabbed at her jumper, came in her wake. Helen brushed her hand irritably loose. 'You're getting good,' she said to the boy. She pointed. 'I especially like that one.' Russell had helped the boy sculpt a face on the side of a bowl. She turned to Jade. 'It's obvious where you'd prefer to be, so I wonder if perhaps your brother and sister might like to come over and play? Maybe tomorrow afternoon?'

'Thanks.'

Russell didn't hear more than polite acknowledgement and neither did Helen. She waited, then was forced to shrug. 'Okay, we'll just leave it with you. But the invitation's there.' She turned to find Russell. 'We'll get out of your hair, let everyone get back to what they're doing.'

Lucy, head down, walked fast to the door. Russell, baffled, followed the girl and her mother outside to apologise. Jade and

Emma had reverted to a coldness he had, over the last few days, almost forgotten.

'I'm sorry, Helen, I don't know why they weren't a bit more forthcoming. It's just they've got quite involved in the clay. Emma does like computer games, though, like your two.'

At the name, Lucy detached herself from her mother's side and sprinted across the cropped grass towards the corner of the house, and the road. Caught by the suddenness, he and Helen halted and stared after her. The girl was flying, vanished. Helen shook her head. 'I have no idea what that's about.' She turned to him. 'Anyway, they'll come or they won't. Don't pressure them. I just thought you might like a break.'

'Oh I'm still managing to work. But thank you.'

Jade was on her own. She spoke without taking her eyes from the cylinder rising on the wheel-head. 'They went over to watch telly.'

The boy had left a bowl with a coil half-attached and two more coils on the slab. Russell picked up the sheet of plastic that had kept the clay from drying out over lunch and covered bowl and coils. She cut the cylinder from the wheel-head and lifted it onto the ware board beside her other three keepers, then wiped her hands on the smeared half-towel that lay across her thigh.

'Em was feelin a bit weird. She gets these headaches. I'll go over and see.'

'I thought she seemed … not herself. Perhaps television isn't a good idea. I'll come and find her a Panadol.'

'Nah, she don't take nothin, it goes away.'

'Are you sure? We can give her half a one?'

'Nah. And he wants a bread.'

It took three sievings to get the unctuousness he wanted. When finally the glaze was a slow drip he swiped his hands over the bucket and lidded it and took the sieve and brush out to the tank tap, having to step around the board that had been the girl's table and which was still lying where it had tumbled. He leaned it against the wall where she'd spot it.

He entered the kitchen in his socks. He couldn't hear the television. He walked to the lounge room. The screen was blank. He stood and turned his head, listening for their voices. The house felt empty. Panic rising in his gorge, he half-ran into the other hallway. The door to their room was open. The beds were made, the extra blankets folded and placed on the chair. The sports bags were gone, the yellow rubber boots, the rolled and tied sleeping bags they'd kept piled in the corner. Lying on the foot of the double bed was a page pulled from the phone pad.

Dear Russell

Sorry. Thanks.

All three had signed it, the boy with *t*.

He ran out to the street. The roadway, as much as he could see of it, was empty. He started back towards the house for his wallet and keys, and stopped. She wouldn't have walked them laden with bags and sleeping bags past Helen's. He spun and strode to the lookout.

Their prints were in the fine sand of the corridor that wound through the dwarf casuarinas to the top of the 'well', the tread of the girl's new joggers as sharp as if stamped by the die that made the soles. Jade must have checked escape routes on the first day at the house.

He looked at the sky. He could get down to the creek in daylight, but not back. The morning, then, early. But would he even be able to persuade her to return? Not if she now deemed the house and street unsafe. But she knew Helen had been told about them. Something else, then, had happened. In the workshop, he thought. The two hadn't left to watch television, they'd been instructed to pack. Had that included food? The kitchen would tell him.

The bagged loaf he'd left on the sink to thaw was gone. The fruit bowl looked undisturbed, but they wouldn't have bothered with fruit. He walked to the fridge and was curling his fingers around the handle when the phone rang.

'Hello Russell, it's Helen. Russell, I've got a rather hysterical girl here. It's taken me close to an hour of talking to her through her bedroom door to get her to open it. She says she knows your niece's daughter — Emma. I've tried to tell her she couldn't possibly, she's mistaken her for someone, but right at the moment she's so upset and frightened she's not open to logic.'

'"Frightened"?'

'Yes — for you. She says they're tricking you. She's played her, she says, at soccer. She goes to North Katoomba Public.'

'I see. I think I'd better come over.'

'If you would.'

Her tone was not request. She believed her daughter.

Jerome answered the door. He, too, looked frightened, but probably at this sister he'd never seen before. He pointed down the hallway, but Russell could hear the sobbing and Helen quietly speaking.

They were seated at the kitchen table. The girl was facing the doorway but couldn't see him, her eyes pressed shut, her wet hands clasped on her chin to stop its quivering. On the table was an untouched glass of orange juice. Helen glanced round and jumped up, motioning him to the seat she'd been sitting in facing the girl and pulling out the one beside it. He sat, coughed lightly in case the girl wasn't in a state to have heard the door.

'Lucy? It's Russell.' He shifted in the chair to remove Helen from the corner of his eye. The girl was the one owed the explanation. 'You're right, Lucy, you do know her. She lives in Katoomba.'

'Jesus,' he heard Helen breathe. He kept his eyes on the girl's face.

'Thank you for being worried about me, but they weren't tricking me, they're in trouble, and I was hiding them from the people they're in trouble with. I say "was" because they've gone, a little while ago. Without telling me. I didn't understand why, but I do now, since Mum rang and told me you were upset. She recognised you, too, didn't she — Emma.'

139

The girl nodded. She took a deep shuddering breath and opened her eyes.

He asked the boy, hovering in the doorway, to come into the kitchen and spoke then to them all, giving the true story and apologising for the invented one, but not for its necessity.

'You'd have thought I'd gone silly.'

He declined coffee, but stayed for a further twenty minutes. Helen was quiet, but it was, he thought, an accepting quietness. It helped that on the day the police had come to the lookout she'd seen them too. By the time he stood to go Lucy was calm, murmuring, 'That's all right,' and giving him a flicker of a smile when again he thanked her for having been worried about him.

The house was cold. The last three nights the boy had helped him set and light the heater. He went to the bedroom and put on his heavy jumper. He wasn't hungry, but needed to eat. He took from the fridge the thigh fillets he'd intended to grill. He could do a quick curry. The phone rang. He half-ran, then his hand hovered. It couldn't be her, from down there she had no reception. It was likely Helen with a question.

'Russell, Kayla. She rung me, yeah? That neighbour's kid knew Em.'

'Yes, I've just come back from there. Those people are safe, they could have gone on staying here.'

'Not your call, ay, Jade's. You done heaps, so thanks. Not your fault.'

'What about food again, Kayla? They took a bit, but not enough.'

'Not your worry. They ain't in the same place you found em, so don't go lookin.'

'Have you traced your mum's cousin?'

Down the line came a heavy silence.

'The reason I'm asking, are they going to be down there a *further* two weeks!'

'I don't fuckin need this. Like I said, not your worry.'

'No, Kayla, listen, what I'm getting at, I have a car, you and I could go down to Sydney and you can talk face to face to the people you've been ringing.'

'You done enough. Thanks. Bye.'

He stood holding the beeping handpiece. 'Fuck!' He turned and pulled out a chair, hit the end-call button and laid the handpiece on the table. He would never see them again. He'd not even got to say goodbye. Surely, though, she would ring once they were in Marrickville or wherever. The note, brief as it was, implied that she knew it was nothing he'd done. It was just freakish bad luck. But he'd lost them.

What, though, if she couldn't find the woman — Kayla couldn't? 'Mother's cousin' was barely, he'd have thought, a legal relative. And they'd been born in Katoomba, their sister was here, whatever friends they had were here, they went to school here. Both Kayla and Jade believed, even hoped — from the way they spoke — that their mother would get a gaol sentence.

141

He didn't think Jade would approach her father, she'd called him a prick. Anyway, the young ones weren't his. But she was a minor — by law even if in no other way. They'd *have* to be fostered, all three. He was in Katoomba, he had the means, he had the room, they appeared to like and trust him. Was he eligible? He screeched back the chair and scurried along the hallway to his study.

The Fostering NSW site informed him that he was. The requisites were Australian citizen, in good health, able to obtain Working with Children and National Police clearance. From their *Ten Myths of Fostering* he learned that a foster parent could be single, childless, and, most importantly — for him — *any* age over twenty-five. Of prime importance to the assessors were whether his health, his energy, and his maturity were 'up to it'. They had proven to be for the best part of a week. Why not for a year? Longer if needed, depending on how long their mother got. Jade would probably want nothing to do with her, but he assumed the littlies would have to be returned to her when she was out and back in Katoomba. But for dealing she might get years! And even when she was out they might actually get a choice, whatever their ages. And choose him.

He would, he read, be offered training, 24/7 access to a caseworker, peer support. He didn't need their tax-free allowance. He clicked on the list of agencies and typed in his postcode. Half were, from the names, religiously affiliated. He clicked on the first that wasn't. Creating Links was based in Bankstown but had a branch in Faulconbridge. He went methodically through the list. Only one other was close to being local, in Penrith. He returned to Creating Links and bookmarked it.

He was too excited to eat. He made coffee, drank it pacing. He needed badly to talk to Jade. Why oh why had he not thought to get her number? And a *surname*! Hers, at least. 'Well, you weren't anticipating she'd just … *take off*!' He didn't have a number for Kayla either. He stopped pacing. Her boyfriend — what was his name? Greg! He'd been picked up at the 'Y'. They crashed at the old YMCA, Jade had said. There was no guarantee they'd returned to doing so. But it was the only place he had. He lifted the phone and snatched the book out from under it. There was no longer a YMCA listed for Katoomba. Near the high school, had been her only other clue. He got his keys and the torch from the drawer and went out to the garage.

The directory was too recent. He would have to drive circuits. Even if signage had been removed, an abandoned hostel would be recognisable. And he'd need to be there early. He put the directory back in the glove box.

The first thing he saw when he opened the back door was the chicken thighs. They'd been sitting out on the cutting board for an hour. 'You're getting stupid, my man.' He'd have to sharpen up if ever it came to an interview. He put the thighs back in the fridge. They'd left him enough bread for a toasted cheese sandwich. He ate it standing at the window seats and looking down at the unfinished game, noting as he had each time they'd played that no white piece was placed exactly in the centre of its square.

In bed he watched the boy on their second morning in the house. He was standing, entranced, at the kitchen window. Thirty metres from the steps was the big male wallaby that was here most mornings, with the black stripe down its spine. It was cropping a patch, then moving languidly on its haunches to the next. Hadn't he seen them down at the creek? Russell asked him. Jade answered. 'Nah, we just heard em.' The boy asked could they go outside. 'We can try. But it'll probably hop away.' He still wanted to, took Russell's hand when they started towards the door.

On the landing, inspiration struck him. He whispered to the boy that he would stay out of sight, but the boy should bend over and hop down the steps. He was the same size, the wallaby might think he was a wallaby too. It would stand up, but he should do slow hops and see how close he could get. He had no idea if what he'd said would work, but it did. The boy got to five metres from the animal before it took three sidling hops and halted, ears flicking, to study again this sort-of wallaby. He couldn't get so close a second time, but the wallaby didn't panic, simply hopped to maintain its distance. When the boy's thighs tired he straightened, and the wallaby spun and bounded past the kiln shed and into the tea-tree. The boy watched it go, then turned to find him, his face alight.

He'd watched wallabies with Michael when Michael was the boy's age. Now, lying in bed, he asked himself why, back then, he'd lacked the imagination to tell his son to do the same thing?

The steel sign was pocked by rocks and rusted, but still legible. He drove slowly along the fence line. The complex of single-storey huts occupied the centre of an area of four or five house blocks. Bush left in the corners had recolonised much of the grounds, eave-high wattles and gum saplings growing in the corridors between the huts. He wondered who owned the land, and why it hadn't been turned into units. Holes big enough for a person had been torn in the chainwire fence in three places and well-used pads ran to the openings. He drove back and parked at the widest. The huts had the look of barracks. Every panel in the fibro walls facing the road had been smashed, the louvre windows were louvreless. It wasn't a place he'd have chosen for a winter squat. Anyone camped inside would probably have noted the suspiciously slow-moving car. So did he really need to go in? The place had a brooding, even hostile, feel. 'Yes,' he muttered, 'you do.'

He locked the car and looked along the row of houses opposite. No one was blatantly watching him. But if the police did raids he was probably being observed from behind curtains. He wouldn't have made much of a spy, he should have parked a street away. As if to make a belated claim on guile he turned towards the huts and bent to peer from under his brows across the roof of the car at the same time as he would seem to be looking inside it. Again, no fleeting face at a window. He walked round the car to the opening ripped in the fence — the 'how' interesting him now that he was close enough to see what force had been exerted — then stepped over the ankle-height strand of twisted wire too strong to break and, keeping his eyes on the windows even though believing the scrutiny futile, walked towards the small roofed landing at the end of the nearest hut.

There were four wooden steps. A heavy chain and padbolt hung useless, the timber of the door splintered where he guessed the lock had been removed and the chain run through its hole. He bent and peered through the gap into a pale yellow corridor with doorways each side, then pushed the door, wincing in expectation of a loud rusty creaking. It swung open with a squeak no louder than a wren's.

The internal walls, too, had been smashed. He picked his way along the corridor, trying to step on patches of bare board, but the shards of fibro lying so thickly it was impossible to be silent. Some rooms still contained an iron bedframe with a sprung-wire base or a steel locker battered open, but most were empty, apart from the fibro and glass littering their floors, and in one, bringing him to a halt, a blue bicycle so mangled it looked like an artwork. At the end of the corridor a doorway with hinges but no door opened into a large bare room with bolted double doors and in the left-hand wall a serving hatch. The walls and even the ceiling were a riot of spray-canned graffiti. It was a try-out space, he thought, for walls he'd seen in town.

He turned to his left, and recoiled. Staring unseeing over his head was Che, the iconic image, in black beret and star. He'd been given a haloing of chrome yellow. Beneath in red cursive was sprayed, *It is not necessary to wait until all conditions for making revolution exist; the insurrection can create them.* Russell's spontaneous response was a guffaw — revolutionaries in Katoomba! — followed by embarrassment. A thinker, a fellow reader at least, had squatted here. He looked quickly again round the room, but it was the only political statement, the rest were the usual geometric tags.

The hatch and the room's size said it was a communal dining hall. Which it still was, it seemed. Around a half-sheet of corrugated iron with the remains of a recent fire were stomped beer and Coke cans, barbecue-chicken bags, cracker boxes and bread wrappers, tins with the labels burned off. The smell of curdled milk drifted up from a carton near his feet. There was nothing, though, to sleep on, no dead mattresses or the chunks of raw foam he'd seen down at the overhang. He had a black texta in the glove box. The walls were too busy, but there was space on the floor. A message there would even be more visible. *Kayla. Ring me please. Russell.* No. She'd be angry at being what she'd perceive as stalked.

He nodded to Che, then picked his way back along the corridor to the open door and out onto the landing, pulling the door to by the chain, the hinges giving their wren's squeak. He was almost at the rip in the fence when he was hit between the shoulderblades by the sensation of being watched. It was too strong to ignore. He went through the pretence of spotting a lace undone, crouching to retie it, the while surreptitiously scanning windows from the corner of his eye. Too long crouched would give away that he knew. He stood and walked to the rip. The sensation didn't abate, persisting to the car, and shifting to the back of his head as he drove away.

He rang and got Hugh. He told him his visitors had left and asked if he wanted to come over tonight, or would he prefer to wait till Thursday, keep things in sync.

'No fear, I'll be over! Only be watching crap on the box. So where'd they go?'

'Tell you tonight. Love to Del.'

He went to the workshop and lit the heater and while it caught cleared the table of the tools and the boy's unfinished bowl and unused coils and took the marble slab out to the tankstand. Then he turned the feet of the blossom jars he'd thrown a century ago — how it felt.

The jars couldn't have been left, but when he'd carried the last to the racks he closed down the heater and fetched his leather-faced gloves from the annexe and wheeled the barrow over to the wood stacks. Which was where Helen found him. She apologised for not having come over sooner, the hardware had called her in for someone off with flu. He was loading splits from the oldest row of radiata. He knocked a test pair together, flipped them into the barrow, the habit so engrained it was no longer conscious, but she stopped speaking.

'What does that do?'

'What? Oh — the ring. For dryness.' He suddenly remembered — Lucy! — took off his gloves. 'How is she?'

'She's fine. I was more concerned about you. Have you heard anything?'

'Their older sister rang to thank me, and to tell me my services were no longer needed.'

'They're back hiding, then.'

'I gather so, yes.' He didn't say how he'd gathered, that he'd found their prints at the lookout.

'Well, at least she thanked you. Which is something, considering the risk you ran.'

He watched her face. She wasn't embroidering. 'With whom?'

'DoCS. Or whatever they call themselves now. They can prosecute you. For hindering an operation. Even more likely where they've called in the police.'

'I didn't realise they could go as far as laying charges. But I suppose … being a government body.' He gave a tight laugh, looked down at the scarred and sap-stained gloves. 'Not that knowing would have changed anything.' He slapped the gloves against his hand as a punctuation. 'I forgot to ask the other day — how's the work going?'

'You mean yesterday.'

'Yes. Sorry.'

'That's all right, a bit's happened. It's going well — I've finished another one and halfway through a new one. Should have enough by the deadline to give me a choice.'

'Always a good plan.'

'Yes.' She took a step back, nodded towards the barrow. 'I didn't come over to hold you up, I just wanted to know if you'd heard anything. The other thing — sorry — but Lucy's worried now about Emma. Where's she sleeping, does she have enough to eat, et cetera. I know, the same questions you'd be asking yourself.'

'They took food from here. Tell her that.'

'Okay, good, I will. She also said to tell you she's very tough to play at soccer. Emma is.'

A laugh forced itself out. 'I don't doubt it, just playing her at chess. She's pure will, that one.'

He barrowed and stacked ten loads at the firemouth. It was enough to dull thought, work off his restlessness. He crossed the grass to the laundry and pocketed the brush and cloth.

It was a shorter time than usual between visits, but the jars were powdered as thickly as ever. He cleaned Michael's first, then hers, walked to the edge and whipped the cloth clean, then folded it around the brush and pushed the bundle into his pocket. He moved the white pebble marking his spot and sat, rested his left hand on the lid of her jar.

'You'd have liked them. Not just the boy, all of them. They're not tame.' He stroked a finger down the jar to feel the fissures in the guan. 'Helen tells me I could have faced charges. Still could, I suppose. But they'd have to be caught first. Anyway, I'd reckon they're pretty good liars.' The ledge faced south, sunless even in summer. He felt in his pocket for the hanky and pinched the bead of snot from the tip of his nose. 'This surprised me — but even at our age we were eligible to foster them. All you have to be is healthy. And not a crim. Which we might have managed to establish.' A shiver bit his neck, ran down his spine. 'That wasn't you, it's getting cold.' He pinched his nostrils again and stood. 'Only thing, they'd have moored us here. But anyway, they're looking for a so-far elusive cousin of their mother's. Just have to hope she isn't cut from the same cloth.' He leaned and kissed her lid. 'Better make a move, I've got Hugh coming.' He picked up the white pebble, set it back in its place, his place.

Hugh arrived at seven with a bottle of the organic red from Orange he and Delys drank by the carton. He plonked it on the table and dived a hand into the pocket of his lumber-jacket, pulled out test rings threaded on his index finger, and slid them clinking softly onto the table beside the bottle. 'Check these. Taken a page out of your book. That's a slip from a clay I spotted in the sewer trench they're digging for the neighbour's extension. She salts, mate!' He singled out and lifted to the light one of the rings, 'Look at this!', held it out to Russell to take. The salt had drawn from the slip a rich rust with gold spangling, the texture a fine-pored orange peel. Russell placed the ring back on the table and examined the others. They were good, but the first was the star.

'I hope you marked where you took it from.'

Hugh laughed. 'Better — snuck in and dug a bagful. They'll notice their trench's got a belly, but they'll be scratching their heads for the why!' He spun and headed for the shelf with the wine glasses.

'Don't get too cocky, you've hardly outdone yourself, your neighbour's backyard.'

Hugh laughed again, too thrilled with his find to be chastened. He broke the seal, poured their glasses, handed one to Russell. He took a sip and sobered. 'You were a bit cryptic on the phone, old son. I said to Del, something's happened.'

He told him what the 'something' was.

Hugh was silent for a few seconds. 'I can't say I know Helen, but she didn't strike me as the dobbing type. So where were you?'

'Like I said — the workshop. They'd been there *with* me. I went over the house an hour or so after Helen left, and they were gone. Wrote me a note, thanks and goodbye.'

'Hah. Trusting little souls.'

'Me, I think they were starting to.' He picked up the bottle by its neck, ushered Hugh towards the bay window. 'You'd have liked the younger girl — Emma. She spotted the board the first night, wanted to know what it was. A day and she was into it, playing a full game. She fell in *love* with the travel set, even took it to bed.'

'You're lucky she didn't knock it off.'

He kept to himself that he'd had the same thought.

Geoffrey rang. He was writing the ad to go into *Art Almanac*. He *was*, he hoped, still able to list Russell?

'They're made. I'll be firing in a month.'

'Ah. I think last time we spoke it was a month.'

Once he'd have felt the need to apologise.

'Still gets them to you in time, Geoffrey.' A spasm of crossness, though, at manipulations earlier in their dealings, made him mischievous. 'Barring mishap.'

Geoffrey didn't rise to the bait. The glaze kiln was now almost an extension of Russell's hands and brain. The teapots would come from it if not perfect then near.

'Will you need the courier, or …?'

'Hugh'll bring them.'

'I'll very much look forward to seeing them.' *And saving on the freight*, Russell added silently. 'Can you email me description and prices.'

The three had put a dent in his schedule. A few early starts and long days would put him back on track. He refused anymore to work at night. He cleaned the blackboard and took inventory of the racks, chalking on the board what was still needed and their quantities. Always needed, and always left so late they went in dubiously dry and risked exploding, were the fillers. He would be good and make them now.

He threw fingerbowls off the hump, gave them feet he moulded immediately with his thumbs. The kiln ate them up, and he threw and moulded without bothering to count. The wistful thought came, though, that if the littlies were here he'd have done as the Chinese did and given them the feet to do. When he'd thrown and footed the last, the first could be handled. He dashed iron onto each with a brush, dipped it in shino. Next day he threw the vertical fillers. These short narrow cylinders he didn't name — vases, pencilholders, he didn't care what use they found. They, too, got a slash of iron, would get, when they were dryer, the limestone that gave a pale celadon. Lastly, again off the hump, he threw thirty eggcups — his nod now in every firing to Adele — to be stamped with the sun orchid he'd carved, then glazed with ash.

Conscience cleared, he turned his mind and hands to what he still found an exhilarating challenge, tea bowls. And — when the state of concentration necessary to them waned — to readying the kiln — cleaning shelves, patching saggars, filling cracks in the roof arch and, at day's end, more mindless barrowing of wood to the firebox door. In this way he passed five solitary days, speaking to no one but himself and the idiots on the television news, and devising meals from the four-person stockpile in the fridge and pantry.

He'd finished throwing. Ahead of him was a long day of glazing — the blossom jars, the open bowls, the fillers, the teapots. The day after, turn the tea bowls and give each its first coat. And that day he could take his time, work until dark, because, hallelujah!, he didn't have to cook, it was fortnight Thursday, Hugh and Delys's and the breaking of his fast on human contact.

The sky when he woke was low and grey and stayed that way. The annexe was freezing, too cold for wet fingers. He carried his glaze buckets and ladles into the workshop, arrayed them in a semi-circle before the heater, and set the low wooden stool within arm's reach of each bucket.

By midafternoon he was on the teapots. They always posed complications — another reason he'd stopped making them — their mouths narrow, the strainer holes needing to be unblocked, lids and rims requiring waxing where they met to keep them free of glaze. He'd melted and brushed the wax, had poured the insides with the thin shino which complemented the guan. He swapped buckets, stirred the guan yet again to combat its liking for settling out, and started once more along the row of eight, two fingers hooked inside the rim of each while he ladled the thick cream, barely liquid, onto its outer walls and spout.

He'd done five, was reaching for the sixth, when the phone rang, startling him from his work trance. Always now when it rang here he was returned to the morning of the hospital. He breathed in, held it, out, then hooked the ladle and stood, swiped his hands down his trousers. He made himself not hurry, it would be Hugh, or an Indian woman in a call centre wanting to sell him a better plan.

'Russell speaking.'

'You're there, good! It's Kayla. Toddy's sick, chuckin up and shittin. We're bringin him. In an hour. Don't tell no one.'

'What?'

The handpiece burred in his ear.

An hour! Chucking and shitting? He needed to go to emergency! That's what he'd say — not even let them in the door, drive them straight there. He dropped the handpiece in the cradle, spun to face the quiet semicircle of buckets, the stool awaiting his return. First, lid the buckets, you don't want to be kicking any over. He snatched up the stool and plonked it down out of his way, then, barely letting them drain, gathered up the ladles and dumped them in the sponge bucket and placed and clipped lids. He glared around him — clean sheeting, clean sheeting! He found some, flicked it open, and covered the teapots, tucking each into its own cell. God only knew when he'd be back! He looked at the window — it was already getting dark — at the dusty clock face — half-four. She wouldn't care that she'd said an hour, they could be here any minute. He spun

closed the heater, took a last wild look around the workshop —
nothing — dashed for the door.

He stripped on the landing, strode in underpants to the
shower. He kept it short, on his naked way to the bedroom
ducking into the study and switching on the computer.

Dressed, he googled 'child — vomiting and diarrhoea'.
The boy had gastroenteritis. It was common, could be viral or
bacterial. He looked at the photo gallery on the wall and found
his favourite, he holding a well Michael and Adele hugging
them both. He had no memory of dealing with gastro. Anyway,
whatever had been the practice then would be years out of date.
He returned his eyes to the page. The parent shouldn't panic,
in most healthy children the immune system controlled both
the vomiting and diarrhoea within twenty-four hours. The
parent should, however, be alert to the risk of dehydration. Mild
symptoms were dry mouth, sunken eyes, weakness. More severe
were lethargy and confusion, pale or mottled skin, fast shallow
breathing, fever. In such cases rehydration drinks containing salt
and sugar, and available in sachet form, should be given. The
parent should, however, be aware that severe dehydration was a
medical emergency and hospitalisation generally advised. *Parent,
parent*, the page kept repeating. The word assumed experiential
knowledge he no longer possessed. He jumped up and hurried
to the kitchen, found the number on the list on the wall.

Lucy answered. No, mum was at work. 'Do you want her
mobile?'

He glanced at the list. 'Thanks, I have it.'

Helen answered on the second ring. 'Yes, Russell?'

He'd never rung her mobile. He heard she was alarmed but trying to not sound so. He apologised for ringing her at work.

'I'm not, I'm walking to the car. What's happened?'

'Ah ... in a minute ... I just wanted to ask first if Lucy or Jerome have ever had gastroenteritis.'

'Both. Name me a school-age child who hasn't. Why are you asking?'

He told her.

She was silent. He could hear her breathing, and the rhythmic tap of what might have been an earring.

'Russell, I'm at the car, just let me get in.' The phone bumped on metal. There was a mysterious pause, and she came back on. 'Okay. What do you want me to do?'

'Can you be on call? If I can put it that way? I really don't think I'll be able to persuade them to let me take him to hospital if that's what he needs, or even call my doctor. If I try to insist I really do think, on past experience, they'll just bundle him up again and go.'

'You've been on Google, I take it?'

'Yes.'

'Lucy was touch-and-go whether she went to hospital, but didn't. I'm pretty sure I've still got the proper rehydration stuff. I doubt it dates. So. Still don't know what they'll say, though, do we? To involving me. But yes, I'm happy to be on call. I'll be home in ten.'

Out of respect for Jade's paranoia he didn't turn on the porch light. He got a blaze going in the heater, then closed off rooms to channel the warm air into the guest room and bathroom. He made up the double bed and carried in two armchairs. But they would be for later. He had a strong memory of a hideous night in Hangzhou when he'd lain on towels on the tiles of the hotel's bathroom alternately throwing up and shitting, and his wonder of a wife, ignoring his pleas to leave him in his foulness, had gently hosed and sponged his arse and thighs. The memory took him to the linen press. At the very bottom he found the cache from which she'd drawn the seemingly endless supply of cheap towels she'd used when painting. He counted out six and carried the stack to the bathroom, placed it on the floor. Then he went to the laundry and fetched the plastic basin and left it, too, on the bathroom floor. He couldn't even contemplate eating. He made a full plunger.

He was on his second mug when he heard footfalls on grass. A hoarse whisper — Emma! — floated up to him, 'I can smell coffee, he's in the kitchen.' *Your senses are extraordinary, little girl,* he said silently as he rose and darted for the door. She had been sent ahead to knock, was on the top step. She gave him a shy pleased smile, quickly muted to the seriousness of the visit. 'Hi, Russell.'

'Hello, Emma.'

Jade was behind her, in her arms the boy swaddled in an opened sleeping bag. She nodded. He stepped out of her way.

'The bathroom, it's ready.' Emma had stopped to take off her joggers. 'Leave them, just come in.' He looked down the steps. 'Where's Kayla?'

'Comin.'

And as she spoke Kayla appeared in the light falling onto the grass. He looked behind her for the shadow boyfriend, but she was alone. She was in the same black studded jacket. She bounded up the steps like an animal.

'Thanks, yeah.'

'The bathroom. Emma, show her.'

While waiting he'd spooned honey into a mug and stood the spoon. He poured in warm water from the jug, stirring as he hurried along the hallway. The door was pushed to, not to exclude him, he discovered when he pushed it open, but because she'd remembered the bar heater mounted on the wall. He contracted his nostrils, but the smell entered his mouth. She and Kayla were kneeling each side of the spread bag and stripping him. The room was already warm, and she'd removed her windcheater, and Kayla the leather jacket. The boy's trackpants and underpants and the blue nylon of the bag were wet with shit, his windcheater streaked with vomit. His eyelids were fluttering, and he was moaning at being jostled. His face was even more pinched than Russell remembered, and white as the tiles. He snapped from his stare when he saw Kayla glancing round for where to put the fouled clothes. He handed Emma the mug and picked up the top towel from the stack and opened

160

it between the boy's feet. 'Drop everything on here, I'll get rid of it. And the bag when he's off it.'

'We're puttin him in the shower, yeah,' Jade said, not looking up from trying to draw one leg of the trackpants over the foot without smearing it too with shit. 'Can you start it, please.'

Emma shuffled out of his way, the mug cradled in both hands. He nodded down at the floor, 'I don't think it's needed right now, maybe put it in that corner.' He leaned into the cubicle and turned on the hot, waited for it to come through, then the cold, and balanced them at a little above warm. When he turned the boy was naked and they had a hand under each armpit and were lifting him. Russell's mind flew to his youth, skinned rabbits. The boy hung limp, head down, his greasy hair flat to his scalp. Kayla seemed awkward. He stepped to slide his own hand into the armpit she was holding, and she snapped, 'I got him, move!' He retreated, offended despite himself. Emma caught his eye, *just let her*. Jade said mildly, 'Take this arm. I'll wash him.'

She had finished, asked Emma to pass a towel from the pile, when the boy groaned and tried to lift both feet and a pale brown stream squirted down the backs of his legs and swirled on the tiles of the cubicle. He began to cry. 'Sorry, Jadey.'

'It's all right, we know you can't help it.' She was already reaching again to the flannel and soap.

Russell couldn't tell whether the boy even knew where he was, that the male voice he was hearing was his.

'Todd, it's Russell. I've had the sickness you've got, everyone has. It's horrible, I know, and it's scary, but it'll stop, okay, I promise.'

They were able to lift him clean from the cubicle, stand him on a folded towel. Jade began to dry him. She gave a light cough, didn't look up. 'We left our bags. Have you got any clothes from ... you know ...?'

'No. I'll get him a tee-shirt of mine. And a sloppy joe — you can roll the sleeves.'

She looked up, gave a flicker of grin. 'Better be old ones, yeah.'

'I think for the moment it's best you sit him on the toilet with a towel round him. And ... then we need to discuss what we're going to do.'

Kayla changed grip on the boy and spun. 'Ain't doin nothin! He's stayin here!'

'Which is what I thought you'd say. But you know as well as I do, Kayla, where he *should* be.'

'No fuckin way! Can't give em a bullshit name, they run it through the computer. His real one's on there, he's been in before. They'll go straight to the fuckin cops!'

'Well I've never treated gastroenteritis before, which is the name for what this is, and neither have you. But living just across the road is someone who has.' From the corner of his eye he saw Jade's movements stop, her face tilt up to look at him. He glanced to include her. 'She knows who you are, because

I had to tell her, and you know why. You took off before we could tell you she had no intention of going to the police. She still doesn't.' He let that sink in. 'How long has he been sick?'

Jade spoke at the floor. 'Two, three days. Around that.'

'And has he drunk anything?'

'Yeah, but he spewed it up.'

'Well he's dehydrated, Jade. Please, Kayla, at his age it's serious. I'm going to the bedroom and get those shirts, and you have a talk.' He lifted a finger towards the switch on the wall. 'That other button's the exhaust fan if you want it.' He crouched and bundled up the towel with the befouled clothing. Quickly Jade rolled the sleeping bag on itself, offered him clean fabric to grip it by. He carried both bundles to the door, which Emma opened for him, but without meeting his eye.

He gave them plenty of time. He went first to the laundry and shook both bundles down into the empty machine and poured in two buckets of water. Coming back through the kitchen he drank off as if it were a shot glass the half-mug of tepid coffee. He fed the heater by the light of its flames, then walked to the windows and with two fingers made a slit in the curtains. The roadway was the portrait of emptiness he saw every night. No boyfriend standing sentry. He flicked the curtain closed.

He searched in his work-clothes drawer and found a tee-shirt without holes, and a flannel shirt with most of its buttons. With them in his hands he walked, placing his feet softly, along the hallway towards the closed door. It was heavy timber, was perhaps muffling whatever discussion was still going on. But from behind it came silence. Something had been decided. He knocked, and it was opened immediately. Emma had been waiting. Swathed from hips to chin in towels, the boy was seated on the toilet. His eyes were closed, and he appeared to be drowsing. Jade sat on the rim of the bath supporting him, the mug of honeywater balanced on her thigh. Arms folded, Kayla leaned against the stub wall separating bath and shower cubicle. She didn't look at him. Jade nodded.

'Yeah, ring her.'

'Okay.' He swallowed the temptation to say more, held out the shirts to Emma.

Helen stayed till one. The boy was in the bed and sleeping. Jade, eyes half-slitted, was sitting wrapped in a blanket in one of the armchairs. Her sisters were asleep under a shared doona on cushions on the lounge room floor. Russell walked Helen out to the road.

'I hope you don't have to work tomorrow.'

'No.'

'He seems a bit better for having kept the fluids down.'

'It could all still come back. Are you going to sit with him, too? She looks knackered — Jade.'

'Yes, I'll try to get her to lie down. Tending kilns makes you good at sitting up all night.'

They'd stopped at the bridge over the ditch gutter.

'Our friend Kayla's a bit fierce.'

'She's been out in the world for longer. I still don't know where she lives. According to Jade, they break into weekenders, she and the boyfriend.'

'They can't do that every night. They must have a roof somewhere.'

'"Crashing at Flynnies" was the last I heard. Overheard. Emma didn't approve.'

'She's a sweetie.'

'Yes. She is.'

Helen made no move to go. She knew he hadn't walked her to the road solely out of politeness.

'What?'

'It's cold. This could wait till tomorrow.'

'Well, obviously it couldn't.'

He made the cough that custom dictated presage the slightly mad or dangerous. 'In order of succession, the fathers are "a prick", dead, and in gaol for dealing. Where, as you know, their mother also is, and will be, almost certainly, for quite some time, most likely years. There's been no mention of any other relative apart from a mother's cousin who's left where she was and they can't trace her. Under the circumstances — would you think it foolish ... to be contemplating, at least — making enquiries about ... fostering them? Not Kayla, Jade and the other two.'

Breath exploded from her mouth in a white cloud, 'Fostering?' She flicked her head as if to shake the word from her ears. 'Russell, "foolish" doesn't come near. I think, yes, this conversation would be better had tomorrow.'

'I haven't mentioned it to them, of course.'

She took a step away. 'I need to go. Wash your hands a lot. I'll say just this, though — you'd be getting their histories as well — all those you've just listed, plus Kayla and her friends — and there could be some real doozies there ... It's a step into the proverbial quicksand, Russell. Goodnight. I'll pop over in the morning.'

The boy woke at first light and said he needed to go to the toilet. Russell and Jade got him up. He was weakly outraged to find himself nappied in a towel. He began to tug at the fold until Jade ordered him to leave it on, did he want to shit on Russell's floor? He was able to walk to the bathroom, hold in the urge until seated. The motions still hurt, he shut his eyes tight and groaned. But after two squirts his breathing calmed, and he announced that he was finished. Was he sure! Jade said. Yes! She tore off and folded paper, but after an attempt to wipe himself his arm fell limp and he sagged on the seat. They helped him off, and Jade walked him to the shower cubicle. Russell glanced into the bowl before pressing the button and was glad to see that the mess held none of the streaks of blood there'd been in the night.

By the time his other sisters woke and came in, he was sitting up in bed drinking the rehydration fluid unaided. He drained the cup and said he was hungry. Jade looked at Russell.

'Can he?'

'I don't know. I might ring Helen. I'll just see what the time is.'

Kayla tapped on her phone. 'Six forty-eight.'

'That's a bit early. I'll have a look on the computer.'

The same page he'd consulted yesterday — he lifted his eyes and sat back in the chair — was it only yesterday? Yes. In fact, not even a full day had passed. He found his place, was assured that the child could and should eat as soon as food was requested. There were no guidelines or prohibitions. He decided something dry.

He did two slices of white toast and cheese melted under the griller, cut them into fingers. The boy wolfed them, asked for more, which he also wolfed, then a muesli bar. By eight-thirty, when Helen came over, he was ensconced on the lounge with the other three, watching cartoons. She observed him for a minute from the doorway, then turned to Russell and shrugged. He made coffee, and they took their mugs out onto the landing and sat on the sunny top step. He told her what he'd eaten.

'Well, that's how fast they can bounce back. Especially if the immune system's been exposed as a matter of course to what theirs probably have.'

'And not just down there.'

'No.'

They fell silent. He knew what she was waiting for. But he'd decided not to reopen what he'd begun at the roadside. It was a conversation he needed to have with himself and — depending on what decision he arrived at, and at the right moment — with Jade. Then — and wholly dependent on the answers she gave — with the littlies and with Kayla. Lastly, if it came to it, with the authorities who decided such matters. Grateful as he was to her, he didn't have to justify to Helen whatever decision flowed from those conversations. Nor should he place her in the awkward position that consulting her certainly would. She'd feel bound by what she saw as her responsibility to Adele. To watch out for him. If necessary, save him from himself.

'Do you need to get Jerome and Lucy away?'

'They've already gone. They won't say anything.'

'That wasn't my reason for asking. I thought you might be needed.'

'They've got good at organising themselves. For similar reasons to these four.'

'All the same, if you want to go, I think I'll be all right. He seems to be on the mend.'

She read the wish behind the words. She handed him the empty mug and stood. She descended the steps till their eyes were level. 'Get some advice, Russell, before you go any further. Not just off the net, speak to someone.'

'I need to speak to three people here first.'
'No — last. If at all.'

The boy heard and smelled cooking going on, sent Jade out to
ask could he sit at the table. Russell went in. He had colour in
his face, his eyes were alive and no longer sunk in their sockets.

'Up you get.'

Jade dressed him from the shopping bag Helen had brought.
Emma had been warned, *you tell him they're a girl's and there's
no TV!*

He ate two sausages with tomato sauce and a dollop of
mashed potato, washed down with a glass of milk. Strangely,
though, he didn't want ice cream. Russell, from deep in his
memory, mashed him a banana, sprinkled it with brown sugar.

They watched television while Russell read in the kitchen. He
heard through the door an argument, quickly quelled. Water
ran in the bathroom, then, a few minutes later, the door opened,
and Jade came in.

'He wants to say goodnight.'

Half an hour later she came in again. She'd put on and zipped
her windcheater. Russell closed the book on his finger. 'He asleep?'

'Yeah. Hey, could you drive Kayl and me somewhere?'

'What … now?'

He glanced at the clock. She kept her eyes on him.

'Ain't far. Em's got my mobile.'

He slid the leather gumleaf into the book and stood. 'Let me get my jacket.'

He thought Jade would take the front, but she ceded the place to her sister. Kayla directed him to a clinker-brick house at the older end of Vale Street. A car wrapped and tied like a present sat on blocks on the footpath. At the side of the house was a caravan sporting a satellite dish. Both got out, and Kayla took the lead. On the verandah she knocked and stepped back, shading her eyes. Jade did the same. A blinding spot came on, the door cracked, then opened. The man framed in the doorway looked past them towards the street and studied the car before he unsnibbed the security door. He ushered them past, closed the door. The spot went off, leaving Russell blinking, its after-image emblazoned on his retinas. When it faded he looked for a letterbox, then along the fence, finally at the house façade. There was no number. Did they not get mail? He turned the key in the ignition, read the time, turned it off.

They were inside less than ten minutes, his legs just beginning to feel cool even though his arms and torso were warm in quilted down. Each carried one of the familiar travel bags and a tied sleeping bag. The spot snapped off. He got out and opened the back, but didn't dare offer to relieve either of her load. 'Thanks,' Jade murmured when they'd heaved the bags in onto the mat.

Kayla again took the front. She let him reach the Yeaman Bridge roundabout before she spoke. 'Not Bathurst Road, yeah, we're goin out the highway.'

He lifted his foot. 'Oh?'

'Not far — near North Katoomba Public — I'll direct you. Turn at the council lights.'

He remained quiet, left her in charge. He couldn't have said how many times — a hundred? — he and Adele — and for a time Michael — had passed the school on the way to Minni-ha-ha.

She directed him into the street beside the school — Mistral — then, halfway along, pointed, 'Now here.' He read the sign, Paris Parade. She didn't give him a number. He drove slowly, adapted now to her last-minute instructions. In the semi-darkness between two streetlights she lifted her hand. 'This'll do. Don't pull over, we'll just get out. Turn off your lights for a sec.' He did as told. He wanted to ask Jade what was going on, but wasn't sure she'd answer. Kayla cracked the door, pulled it to again when the internal light came on. 'Can you just go for a drive, come back in twenty?'

'I suppose so. Back to here?'

She pointed through the windscreen. 'Run in under there, yeah.'

He looked and saw a weeping wattle, beneath it a cave of shadow. She was already getting out, Jade too. Each closed her door with barely a click. He moved off as quietly, and without lights. 'You're learning,' he murmured. He was nervous, yet excited to have been made an 'accomplice'. He had no idea how long the street was, but calculated it must come out near

Minni-ha-ha Road. He realised suddenly he was doing thirty without lights, snapped them on. Cars and utes, a crane-truck, were parked both sides. Few houses were dark, but he passed not a soul, even a dog. He had not been to Minni-ha-ha since she died. He could drive down to the falls reserve, come back up via one of the avenues. That would use ten minutes. Or park and listen to the radio. 'Or both.'

He returned exactly on time. The street was unaware still of anything happening. He ran in under the wattle and turned off the lights. It *was* like a cave. He watched through the windscreen, did scans of the mirrors. Even so he didn't see them arrive. They were suddenly at the back of the car, the hatch was being sprung. The internal light came on. 'Fuck,' Kayla laughed, 'turn it off!' Jade giggled, smothered it. He was half out. He stretched to the slide switch and thumbed it.

They had the hatch raised and between them were lifting a bulging pink and blue nylon zip bag onto the tray. A second bag, equally crammed, was on the gravel. He stood and watched, they didn't need his help. Jade was still suppressing giggles, which set Kayla off. She clapped a hand to her mouth, snatched it away, hissed, 'Fuckin shut up,' but the words coming out as laughter. He remembered the same nervy laughter after he and his brother scampered through the 'haunted house' on Hat Hill Road. The sisters bent as one and lifted the second bag in beside the first, shoved it against the back seat.

'Is this it?'

Kayla sobered. 'Nah. We'll do it, but.'

They disappeared behind the wattle, weren't away long enough to have gone into a house. Kayla was carrying a black ghetto blaster and a naked guitar, one of its strings broken and dangling. Jade lugged a soft plastic suitcase so distorted it looked as if a child was inside, and a cardboard tube of the kind that held prints or posters. She was struggling, and Russell stepped forward and took the suitcase handle, which she gladly relinquished. Kayla laid the guitar gently on the back seat, put the ghetto blaster on the floor. 'One more,' she said, not looking at him. The giggling was gone.

They came carrying between them, of all things, an electric oil heater, and under their arms and slung round their necks blankets and towels. He didn't think the heater would fit but they rammed it against the bags and lowered the hatch. Kayla got in the back, Jade in the front, the reversal explained when he heard behind him a hollow knock, then a strummed chord, abandoned when obvious how out the strings were.

'Your old house,' he said when they were moving.

'You don't need to freak,' Kayla snarled from close behind his head, 'no one's livin there, it's bein done up. Arsehole agent just chucked everythin in the garage.'

He spoke at the mirror. 'What, you received some sort of notice, or ...?'

'I *come* here, seen it! Bastard'll be fuckin sorry, too, when his windows cop a couple of bricks!'

'Um — could I ask that you leave that for a while? I think we've got enough going on, don't you, without the police looking for you for that too.'

'Fuckers wouldn't know where to start!'

He drew breath to say, *well they picked up your friend Greg*, felt a gentle tap on the knee.

'Kayl, chill, ay. Arsehole could've took it to the tip.'

They were up before him, sprawled like puppies on the couch, already watching cartoons, the salvaged blankets wrapped about them and the electric heater going, its mystifying retrieval now explained — their solution to the morning's dead fire. He said nothing, his power bill each quarter now so low it was almost negligible.

Where, though, was Kayla? He'd been to the bathroom. She wasn't in the kitchen. He walked back to the lounge room.

She'd gone. And her guitar.

They resumed coming to the workshop, Emma too. The distorted suitcase had contained not only clothes, but Lego and CDs and shoes. She now owned a second, shabby, pair of joggers. Jade had exclusive use of the wheel, he was glazing. The pair of cylinders she'd left in the racks were now bone dry. He asked would she like him to glaze them. He couldn't promise there'd be space in the kiln, but if there was he'd fire them.

'Um. I was gonna try and make bottles.'

'Yes, but we don't know how long you'll be here. These are ready.'

She slid from the saddle and came to the racks. He'd moved the cylinders to the front. She stared at them. He read her thoughts. I want something that's finished. I maybe don't want it to be these. He made the decision for her, the one that also suited him. 'They'll fit easier than bottles.'

She stared for a further few seconds, though, before she nodded. She glanced at him, looked back at the racks. 'Can I have like your old bowl? Hare's fur?'

'No. They'd need to go in saggars, and I can't spare any of them. But we can use the same glaze, from the dyke, and you'll get a nice shiny black with some spangles. You happy with that?'

She shrugged.

Wow, he said silently. *Don't know the meaning of 'compromise', do you.*

'Can I dip em?'

'Watch me, then you do the other one.'

Emma was again invited over to Helen's and this time went. After she left, Todd whined to Jade, why just her? She didn't even slow the wheel. 'First you're a boy, second you're too young, third she don't want your fuckin germs.'

He rang and got Delys. He told her the kids were back. Could she tell Hugh, and to ring beforehand if he was coming over rather than just turn up. They were okay now with Helen, but he wasn't sure how they'd react to the unannounced arrival of a white Hilux.

'So they're still that feral?'

'They're not "feral", Del — they're just on high alert. With pretty fair reason.'

'What are they doing back? You thought they'd skipped for good.'

He told her.

'And … is he all right?' Her baiting tone was gone, she was a mother again. 'I could ask Andrew to take a look at him, no names, no pack drill.' Russell had met her doctor son-in-law and liked him.

'I did think of Andrew, but I didn't like to ask. It might've put him in a difficult position.'

'There's ethics and there's family, Russell.'

'Still … Anyway, he's over the worst. The squits have stopped, and he's eating and drinking.'

'Good.' She was silent a moment. 'So … any chance of meeting these characters?'

'I … can ask. Jade would probably be interested in seeing another workshop. If we popped over at night. I'd like to see how she goes on an electric wheel. Just, if it's the littlies as well I might have to choose my moment.'

'They've certainly got under your skin, these three, haven't they?'

It was a perfect invitation to tell her how much. That he'd been reading up on fostering. Fear stopped his tongue. To Del, men were hopelessly the creatures of sentiment.

176

'The place we met I think had a fair bit to do with that.'

He heard he'd confirmed her belief. She said mildly, though, 'I'll pass on the warning.'

The boy was watching television. Jade and Emma were in their room with the door closed listening to rescued CDs. He was washing up. He heard a song stop mid-line, took no real notice until he heard the door open and a moment later the front door. Her mobile. He issued himself the same reminder, *you are not her keeper.*

He and Emma were in the window seats with the board between them when the front door opened again and closed. He wasn't wearing his watch. She'd been gone, though, he thought, about two hours. He heard her speak to the boy and the television go off. Then she was in the hallway, the boy in tow. She evaded his eyes, hooked her head at Emma, *the bedroom, now.* He was shocked to see that she'd been crying.

It was his move, but he wouldn't make it without the girl. He stood and went into the kitchen, filled a saucepan rather than the briki with milk — he'd have chocolate too — put it on the burner, fetched down four mugs and the powder. By the time he'd filled the mugs they were still not out. He would have to go to their door with the tray and knock. He placed the tray on the table, was positioning the mugs for balance, when the door opened, and he heard them come along the hall. They filed silently into the kitchen. The boy and girl stood against the fridge, heads down, attempting to be invisible. A glance at Jade told him why. She was no longer upset, she glittered with anger, a hardness in her eyes and especially about her mouth that took him back to their first few seconds of acquaintance, when she'd given him the merest of nods and swept the scree with her gaze before stepping down onto the overhang floor.

'Me and Kayl've had a fight, a big one. She wants us to go to this bloke named Reb and his missus, yeah, but I said no way. He's another fuckin druggie. I told her we're stayin here and she needs to keep tryin. She bloody lost it, was swearin at me, tellin me I'm not their mother. I told her I fuckin *am*! *I'm* the one with em day and night! It's not *her* livin in a cave, jumpin every time a branch falls or somethin. Havin to get Toddy back up top chuckin and shittin! That's *me* doin that, not her!' She swung her head, looked away at the windows. 'Sorry, I don't need to be yellin this at you, supposed to be just tellin you.'

'What happened with your mother's cousin?' he said quietly.

'Couldn't find her.' She'd calmed. 'She just pissed off, yeah, without tellin no one.'

The time was wrong to open the subject of fostering. She was too raw, the littlies were there.

'Well you stay here till you do. Okay?'

'Thanks.'

He instituted 'recess', all downing tools at ten-thirty for, in his case coffee, in theirs Milo, the four of them seated in a row on the workshop apron with the sun on their outstretched legs. They'd been back inside for five minutes — Jade again on the wheel, the boy coiling a box, Emma sponging run glaze from the bases of the eggcups Russell was dipping — when the phone rang. He stood, wiping his hands on the rag of towel which had lain on his knee. The urgent voice came while he was still drawing breath to say hello. 'Russell — Helen. Two police cars and another car just passed my place and are pulling up outside yours.'

'O Jesus.'

He was speaking to burring.

All three were statues, except for their eyes. 'The police are here.' Jade slid backwards fast from the wheel saddle. 'Please, Jade, don't do anything silly. Go with them, and we'll do everything possible to get you back here, *living* here, *fostered* here! I promise. So please, all sit down and I'll go and talk to them.'

He stepped through the door to the same view of the house that met him every day. For a second he dared hope that Helen had mistaken the cars' markings. Then over the roof came a hammering. It was quicker to go round. He broke into a shuffling run and found the rag of towel still in his hand, threw it backwards towards the workshop. At the corner of the house he almost collided with a uniformed constable and a blonde woman in jeans and a green jumper. Both jumped back, the constable's hand raised in an involuntary *whoa, keep your distance!* Russell halted. The man looked quickly past him, returned his eyes to Russell's.

'Morning, sir, are you the occupant of these premises?'

'Yes, I'm the owner.'

'And you are, sir?'

The hammering stopped.

'Russell Bass.'

'Well, Mr Bass, I'm Senior Constable Carrick and this is —' he opened a hand towards the woman without looking at her — 'Ms Kells, an officer of the Department of Family and Community Services. We have a search warrant if needed, and I'm formally warning you that you're required under the Care Act to answer any questions put to you. Is that understood?'

'Yes.'

'Good. Ms Kells.'

'Mr Bass, we've received a report of the presence of children on these premises who the Department have been trying to locate since the arrest of their mother. Those children, Mr Bass, have been declared by a court to be legally in the care of the Minister. Do you have knowledge of the children, and where they currently are?'

'Yes.' He turned and pointed. 'They're in my workshop.'

'Thank you.'

The constable touched him on the arm. 'Come *with* us, please.'

He had closed the door. Now it stood open. He looked past the workshop and into the tea-tree. The woman was in front, keen to get there, the constable behind him.

'I'm sorry, I think they've gone.'

'I hope you're wrong, Mr Bass,' the woman said into the air. 'For their sake and yours.'

He wasn't. A glance told both they weren't hiding, there being nowhere.

'As you can see, they *were* here. The bottle on the wheel is Jade's. The boy was hand-building. That box's his. Emma was helping me glaze. We were doing the eggcups.' They had allowed their eyes to be directed, but both now were watching him. 'I asked Jade to wait in here and not do anything silly. She's frightened, though, that they'll be split up.'

'Is that what she's told you,' the woman said.

'Yes.'

'Well it's not what we do, Mr Bass. We attempt to keep them together. But I'm not surprised she's spun you a tale, I'm very familiar with our friend Jade. You don't fit the profile of "family associate", Mr Bass, if I may say so. So do you mind telling me please how they came to *be* here. I do know her well enough — and Kayla ... I take it she's been a visitor?'

They turned at a knock on the door. A second constable stood there.

'They were here,' Carrick said, 'but they've skipped. Get on the blower to Josh, tell him they could be circling to come out at the lookout. Then I want another four bodies here, to go through this bush at the back. And give that chook run a good search.'

The man nodded, left the doorway. A moment later Russell heard him relaying instructions.

'Yes — to answer your question about Kayla.'

'What I was going to say, they wouldn't have been here if Jade didn't choose to be. So can you enlighten us, please, as to how you come to have them in your house?'

He omitted Helen from his account. And the night drive to Paris Parade. They appeared, he thought, to believe him. The woman asked did he know where she'd been intending to go after here. He was deliberately vague, an aunt somewhere in Sydney. That was all she'd said. Kayla was arranging it.

'No mention of a name, or even a suburb?'

'Not to me.'

The two exchanged a look he couldn't read. The woman took a phone from her shoulder bag and photographed the bottle abandoned on the wheel-head, then the rough box, its last coil half-attached and hanging. She put the phone away and looked around as if noting for the first time what surrounded her.

'You're a professional potter?'

'I am.'

She grunted as if the possibility had never before occurred to her.

Carrick said, 'We'll take a look in your house, Mr Bass, and as part of that we're permitted to remove anything that establishes their presence. While that's being carried out I'd like you to remain here, please. A constable will be with you in a minute.'

'Am I under some sort of arrest?'

'No, Mr Bass, you're not. There's no offence under the Act of harbouring as such. But we'll need to satisfy ourselves as to whether there might be other matters we wish to speak to you about.'

'Nothing of that sort has happened, Constable. I just fed them and gave them a roof.'

The man nodded. 'We'll leave it there for the moment, eh.'

He stood where he was until they left, then squeezed into the gap beside the wheel to the right-hand window and searched the arc of bush he could see. If they were anywhere, that's where they were, in the dense ribbon running between the block and the cliff edge all the way round to the lookout. They hadn't had time or sufficient cover to have run in any other direction but into the tea-tree. She would know they'd be watching the lookout and the well. She'd find them a sinkhole or wallaby lie, hide out till dark. He wondered would she come to the house first, to get clothes and their sleeping bags, ask him for food. He dearly hoped so! He would speak to her properly about fostering. Try to persuade her to stay the night and tomorrow all go with him to this woman Kells to begin the process. He backed out of the gap. Where was this constable? He walked to the door to look through its pane and gave the constable, about to reach for the knob, a minor fright.

The man didn't give his name, behaved as if he'd been entering pottery workshops all his life and had seen enough to last him.

He drew the stool from under the bench and sat looking out the doorway. Russell couldn't sit. He asked the man was it all right if he worked. Permission was a shrug.

He cut her half-thrown bottle from the wheel-head and dropped it in the recycle bucket. He pinched the coil from the boy's box and dropped it, too, in the bucket, then enclosed the box hopefully in plastic and slid it on its batt onto the lowest rung of the racks, to be visible, but out of his way. He sponged clean the marble slab, and the spoon the boy had been using for smoothing. Then he sat to finish glazing the eggcups.

He'd dipped and wiped two when he heard a heavy motor come across the grass and pull up somewhere near the kiln shed. The constable stood. 'Stay here, please.' He went out to speak to the arrivals.

Russell rose and glided to the door and looked through the pane. The constable was talking to four men in sky-blue forage caps and overalls. Even if they failed to find the three, they would certainly find her orchid colonies and the track to the ledge. He hoped if they went onto the lower ledge they had the nous to understand what they were looking at and the decency to leave the urns untouched. The constable turned, and Russell strode back to the eggcups.

By the dusty clock face he and the constable shared the workshop for a silent forty minutes, until a female constable arrived at the door and asked him to come to the house, please, and lock up, he was going to the station.

He was kept waiting in an anteroom with an internal window he couldn't see through, but suspected he could be seen through. For how long, he didn't know, there was no clock. Eventually a man in a suit and tie and carrying a thin manila folder came in, introduced himself — 'Detective Constable Dixon' — and conducted him to a small room with three chairs set around one end of a long table at whose wall end was, he guessed, some sort of recording and filming device. A second man in a suit came in and sat. Russell was asked to identify himself to the lens, then the men did.

The folder when opened appeared to hold little more than a single sheet. The line of questioning was what Russell had expected and prepared himself for, but was conducted in such a half-hearted manner it was plain neither man believed him to be a paedophile.

At the end of what he judged to be three-quarters of an hour the first man, while the other continued to write, thanked him for his assistance and stood and told him he was free to go, a constable would conduct him to the front desk. There, he was asked to take a seat until a car and driver were available. He'd find his own way, he said, and walked up the street to the rank outside the fish shop.

He stood at the sink and drank two glasses of water, then rang Helen, got the machine. He was concluding his message when there came a rapping on the back door. He opened it with the phone in his hand, and she was there.

'I saw the taxi. I know they didn't find them, but any word?' She lifted a finger towards the phone.

'Word? Oh — no, nothing. I was actually just leaving you a message.'

'Well, if you don't mind repeating it.' He was blocking the doorway. She motioned past him. 'May I?'

'Of course, please — sorry.'

'That's okay, you've had quite a morning.' She waited for him to stand the phone back in the charger. When he turned she nodded towards the blackened Atomic still sitting on the cork mat where he'd placed it at breakfast, in another life. 'Shall I make us a coffee?'

'I think I need something stronger.' He opened the dresser and took out the squat black bottle of cognac. 'You?'

'Not this early, I'll settle for caffeine.'

He didn't own a snifter. He poured a wine glass half full and sat. She carried the percolator to the sink and while unscrewing it said over her shoulder, 'So what was your message?'

He took too big a mouthful, had to wait for the burning in his gullet to ease.

'Just that I was back. And if maybe you'd seen anything of them — afterwards.'

She set the halves of the percolator on the sink and lifted a tumbler from the drainer. 'On second thought, I'll join you.'

She sat and slid the tumbler to the bottle. 'Just a mouthful.'

He poured her a good inch, passed the tumbler back. She put the rim to her nose, sipped, blew a quick startled breath. 'Woh, that's strong.'

He wasn't interested, he was waiting.

She saw and lowered the tumbler. 'I watched the whole thing from Lucy's bedroom. They were here for about another hour after they took you. Every time one of them came from behind the workshop my heart was in my throat till I saw he was on his own. The cars all left, but one cop stayed at the corner of your house, just watching. Then a car came back and fetched him.' She was studying his face. 'So … did you and she have some sort of plan? For something like this.'

He shook his head. 'No, but you can bet she did. Just I wasn't a party to it. Jade to the last.'

'So where do you think they are? Would they have made it to the lookout?'

'Not along the road. Adele had her own little track. Jade may have found it. I just wouldn't have thought they had time. I'm assuming they just ran into the bush. But there's not enough places to stay hidden from a proper search. So I truly don't know. My hope is they're back down in the valley, but they've got nothing except the clothes they were wearing. Nothing to eat, no sleeping bags. Or else she's double-bluffed us all and tracked up the back of the houses and by now they're on their way to Sydney. Wherever they are, I don't think we'll see or hear from them again.'

'That's a bit gloomy.'

'No, I'm just being realistic. She doesn't look behind her.'

Helen rolled the tumbler between her palms. 'How ... unpleasant was it, at the police station?'

'Oh, they asked the questions you'd expect. Not really what's uppermost in my mind. I should have spoken to her days ago, not when the hounds were on the doorstep. I doubt she even heard me.'

'What ... so you actually said it to her? About fostering them?'

'Way too late, and too hurried. But yes, I did.'

'Katoomba's not a big place, Russell. There's a good chance you'll see Kayla. You can put it to her, or at least ask if she'll give you a contact.'

He didn't wish to see Kayla again. He'd had plenty of time to think about why the police and the woman had arrived. He didn't need to say any of this. He said instead, both believing it and not, 'She won't stay here. They're all she's got.'

He rang Hugh and Delys and got the machine.

They didn't ring back. They were probably down at Bullaburra being grandparents. Anyway, he'd lost the urge to talk. He lit the heater and while waiting for the flames to build remembered he hadn't eaten since breakfast. Not that he was hungry. But he needed to eat. There was plenty in the fridge, he'd shopped for four only a day ago. The only thing that appealed, being quick, were the dreaded eggs. But not yet. There was enough light if he left now to squeeze in another, again almost certainly futile, examination of the paths around the lookout. He'd need his down jacket.

He pocketed the torch from the bedside table, carried the jacket. He was just into the hallway when he heard the back door quietly open. He froze. A moment later it quietly closed. He drew a breath to call 'Hello?', held it, and listened. His heart, though, was running ahead of his mind, began to thud. He dropped the jacket and padded fast along the hallway in his socks. The door to the kitchen was open, but before he reached it he smelled them!

He had held the boy, never either girl, but all three walked into his arms. He was glad the light was off, so they couldn't see his eyes. The ash reek was in their hair, their clothes, their skin. He breathed it in! The embrace was clumsy, their different heights. He felt Jade draw away and lowered his arms. He'd begun to guess, but said, 'Where on earth were you?'

'In the kiln, the tunnel.'

'Why we stink!' Emma chirped. 'Right up in the chimney end! She made us breathe through our hands so's we wouldn't sneeze!'

'And you've been there this whole time? Till just now?'

'Yeah, waitin for it to be dark. We could see the sky up the chimney.'

'I nearly sneezed, but,' the boy said proudly. 'Twice! But I stopped it!'

By Christ, he thought, *you're tough little bastards*. He moved towards the switch for the ceiling spots, pointed towards the sink, 'Well, you'd all better have a drink of water, then head to the bathroom.'

Jade flung out a hand. 'Russell — no! No lights! Em, get the torch —' she flicked her hand at the everything drawer — 'go up the hall and turn off that one.' She swung again to face him. 'First time Kayla and me got put in care they come at night, yeah. You got candles?'

'Yes.'

'Can you get em. Please.'

He didn't argue. He walked into the pantry and groped with his fingers at the back of the shelf he thought them on. They would be there, Adele had loved candlelight. He found two boxes, one unopened, the other with five new ones and a stub. He brought both boxes to the table, took down the pair of crystal candleholders she'd brought to marriage from her maiden's bedroom, and the salt-fired candle boat of Hugh's with three sockets. He left the stub, stood the five. The boy wanted to light them, and Russell gave him the matches.

Emma came back, made to return the torch to the drawer. 'You'd better keep it out, eh,' Russell said. He left the crystal pair on the table, carried the boat to the shelf above the stove. The new wicks guttered then steadied. He could at last see how much ash they wore.

'And can you lock the door,' Jade said quietly.

He found the key, did as asked.

'And can you sit. Em.'

The girl planted herself in front of him. Her eyebrows and lashes, even the down on her cheeks, were frosted with ash. 'This mornin. Did you mean it? When the cops come. About we can live here.'

'Foster us,' Jade said.

Emma whirled. '*Jade! I'm* sayin it!' She turned again to him, her face too old for eight. 'So … did you?'

With all my heart, he wanted to say. The old vow would confuse her. No, it was his *heart* speaking! He reached and took her hands.

'With all my heart.'

'Good. I want to learn more chess, and her and me want to go back to school. And he has to start, we told him.' Her fingers squirmed. He released her, and she patted the backs of his hands and crossed her wrists at her waist.

'A bit over two years and I'm eighteen,' Jade said. 'So it's just till then. Then they'll live with me.'

'I don't think we have to cross that bridge just yet. We've got a few others first, I think.'

She came with him. 'Yeah, Kells. How pissed was she?'

'Without knowing her, it's hard to say. She didn't seem to be. She was just very cold.'

She nodded, pleased. 'She was pissed. I'm waitin to see her face in the mornin when we all walk in.'

'I'd prefer she was on our side in this process. Don't you think?'

'You're takin us off her case load. What would you reckon.'

He began to grin, quickly suppressed it. She was serious.

'Russell, we stink, we need to have showers.' She pointed to the boat. 'Can we take that one?' He nodded. She ignored the clever curl, lifted it by the hull. She snapped finger and thumb and pointed, and the boy and girl started towards the hallway. She plucked at her jumper. 'We'll drop all these in the bath, then I'll take em to the laundry.'

She turned, and he said, 'Jade?'

The other two halted, looked back at him. She put the candle boat in Emma's hand, gave her shoulder a gentle shove. 'Bedroom first and get clean stuff.' They went unwillingly. She and he watched them to the hallway corner. When they disappeared she looked at him.

'Yeah. Would've been her.'

'I know why, and it's quite the opposite of stupid. She's got problems, I'm well aware of that, but I didn't feel very forgiving when I was sitting in the police station.'

'You sayin you don't want her comin here.'

'I'm not mad on the idea.'

'She's our sister, Russell.'

'And — what … you're happy to let it go.'

'Not happy, but I have to.' She motioned towards the hallway. 'For them, too, yeah.'

You can't pick and choose, he thought, *it's the whole package or nothing.*

'Tell her she's welcome.'

'And what about … if sometimes she needs to crash here.'

He said carefully, 'We can probably manage that. I'm just not so sure about any friends she might want to bring,' Helen's warning flashing in his head, *there could be some real doozies there.*

'Won't be any. Your house, your rules.'

'Well I'll leave passing on that message to you.' The only lightness in the room was the candles. He attempted a smile. 'We might even get her on the wheel.'

She rose to the attempt with an amused grunt, shook her head. 'I don't reckon.'

'I don't either.' He pointed with his chin to the hallway, 'They'll be starting to worry, and I need to invent us some dinner.' He dug in his pocket for the other torch. 'Here, take this.'

When she'd gone he closed his eyes and found the woman's face, Kells. Her manner had been cold, but the eyes not. Play to them. 'Good morning, we're here to lighten your case load.'

You can't say that!

'My oath you can!'

The water pipe was galloping. He hoped they were all in together! He put his hands to his thighs and pushed himself up. He'd bought mince yesterday, for bolognese, but they would arrive from the bathroom ravenous. In the freezer were pizzas, heat-and-eat. They tasted to him like the cardboard they came in, but the three loved them. Their first dinner as a family, it should be a celebration.

He went to the stove and sparked the oven.

Acknowledgements

The quotes on page 7 are from 'Truth in Form: Pulled-Back Simplicity' by Gwyn Hanssen Pigott, *Studio Potter*, 26 (1) 1997.

Roger McDonald and Bette Mifsud read earlier versions of the novel, and, as always, I am in their debt for a fellow writer's and a wise wife's doubts and suggestions.

Jennifer Sharp read a relevant section and gave her expert advice, for which I am deeply grateful.

Simon Reece allowed me to borrow treasured books from his ceramics library, and I very much thank him.

Thank you to my agent, Lyn Tranter, for being a forceful advocate when even the author wasn't sure about a novel with so much clay in it. And for choosing Scribe to send it to!

Finally, to a superb editor, Anna Thwaites, at Scribe, who, with a sure eye, great tact, and the lovely belief that the process should, wherever possible, be fun, saw the manuscript through to publication. Thank you, Anna!